Unchained

A collection of fiction & poetry
by
BRISTOL WOMEN WRITERS

⬣ Tangent Books

First published 2013 by Tangent Books
First Edition of 500 copies

Tangent Books
Unit 5.16 Paintworks
Bristol
BS4 3EH
0117 972 0645
www.tangentbooks.co.uk
Email: richard@tangentbooks.co.uk

ISBN: 978-1-906477-77-6

Design: Joe Burt (joe@wildsparkdesign.com)

Printed using paper from a sustainable source.

Thanks

Bristol Women Writers would like to thank the following people and organisations for their enthusiasm, support and practical assistance in helping us bring *Unchained* to life and into print.

- Andrew Cox, Reading Manager at Bristol Central Library, his colleagues and Bristol Libraries in general.
- Tania Hershman, author.
- Richard Jones of Tangent Books who 'publishes interesting stuff'.
- Joe Burt of Wild Spark Design for beautiful book design.
- Ali and Jari at *Unputdownable* for inviting us to be part of Bristol Festival of Literature.

For the love of words

Profits from the sale of this book will go to the National Literacy Trust.

The National Literacy Trust is an independent charity that works to improve the literacy skills of disadvantaged children and young people to help them reach their full potential. The charity runs projects in disadvantaged communities to motivate children to read for pleasure, improve the communication skills of teenagers in preparation for the workplace and to support families to give their children the best start in life. It also campaigns to raise awareness of the importance of good literacy skills, carries out policy work with government and researches literacy in the UK.

www.literacytrust.org.uk

Contents

Haiku poems by Jenni O'Connor
Factual snippets by Nicola Bennetts

Unchained

Foreword by Tania Hershman

I visited a chained library recently, in Hereford, and was bewitched. Books – with chains? Books considered so precious that they were imprisoned on their shelves, access to them limited? I couldn't reconcile what I was seeing here with my experience, my every-weekend trips as a child to those palaces where, sitting unshackled on shelf upon shelf, stretching far into the distance, were worlds captured between pages, for me to pluck and take home. When I returned to live in the UK after many years away, I experienced that joy all over again – free books! Books so unchained that I could request they set off and travel between libraries just to find me. It's been almost four years and the delight has not worn off. I visit our wonderful Central Library weekly, and when I walk through the doors I breathe out. This is where I am home.

Unchained is a perfect name for this anthology of short stories – and poetry – by members of Bristol Women Writers. These writers have let loose the shackles of their imaginations and take us on journeys through their library-inspired tales, beautifully, poignantly and thrillingly demonstrating how libraries are so many things to so many people, so much more than just shelves and word-containing paper objects.

I prefer not to discuss the stories themselves, best you approach them fresh and unprepared. Rather, here, in their own words, are just a few of the Bristol Women Writers' libraries: 'This roof is broad enough/to shelter mysteries and time,/poetry and photocopiers'; 'Dan understood that *library* was missing from the name of this place for good reason. Peace, reflection and self-improvement were more likely to be found in the toilet block'; 'Original editions from the seventeenth century crowded the walls, right up to a gallery reached by a tiny spiral staircase'; 'Outside, the van has metal walls … But inside, the walls are … lined with paper. Soft, and lined with silence … so many leaves of paper you couldn't count'.

I'd like to include a word about short stories. Anyone who knows me knows that they have a particular claim on my affections. Short stories are in many ways like libraries themselves, small in size yet unbounded in terms of what they can contain and where they can transport you to, as this collection so aptly demonstrates. A cluster of stories between the covers of a book contains a galaxy of experiences, voices, places, emotions, individuals, communities, connections (and this one even donates its profits to the National Literacy Trust, so you are not only enriching yourself by buying and reading it).

Don't dash through this book. Find yourself a quiet library-like spot, settle down, sink in. As the great Doris Lessing once said, 'A library … is the most democratic of institutions, because no one – but no one at all – can tell you what to read and when and how.' May books never again be chained.

400 Years

Shirley Wright

Its books were chained once –
186 chains ordered
from the local ironmonger
as a deterrent.
    Imagine knowledge being
    so precious, so threatened.

Today we have boldness
and electronics,
the buzz of human thought
that hums between
    Cathedral and City Hall,
    God and Mammon.

Coleridge would have loved
the new Café, tea and muffins
with his mate Robert Southey
who, as Poet Laureate,
    might've found the Internet
    quite handy.

He'd have searched on Wikipedia,
or gorged his passion for words
in the soft fox of paper,
the imprint of ideas
    that spin dust motes
    down the perfume of years.

If there is a ghost, as some
would have us believe, chatter
from the children's corner
will silence him. This roof is broad
    enough to shelter mysteries and time,
    poetry and photocopiers,

prostitutes from the docks, a lock
of Southey's hair, a red
devil's head no fire could destroy.
Once light fell straight from the sky
    down and down to all the dark places.
    That's what libraries are for.

Those Who Would Otherwise Be Cold

Sally Hare

Andrew started off late that day. Long-simmering tension between two of the other tenants had finally boiled over into a slanging match, and everything had been out of whack since. By the time he arrived at Bristol Central Library, his spot on the round table under the stained-glass window had been taken, as had the *Historical World* he had been halfway through reading. It was always annoying when members of the public didn't understand the rules of sheltering in the library. The hostel was not the sort that closed during the day but, like his daily shower and clean shirt ritual, Andrew had always felt that getting out for a regular few hours gave him a bit of structure, kept him part of the world. Also, the heating didn't work very well in the TV room. Sitting here got boring, of course, usually around eleven in the morning, and again at three, but there were worse ways to pass the time, worse places not to think about a drink.

Scanning the long, tiered Reading Room, he discovered his magazine in the hands of a newcomer. She was sitting a third of the way along one of the wooden study benches, a crammed hessian shopper squashed in front of her wellingtons, knuckly fingers turning the familiar pages. It was difficult to guess her age; her clothes were a charity shop jumble, she wore no makeup, and her sandy hair had been pulled into a trend-defying scrunchie at the back. He supposed she could be anywhere between mid-twenties and knocking on forty.

Andrew took a seat as near to the radiator as he could and unpacked: sneaky Kit Kat and the usual packet of cheese sandwiches hidden under his A4 notebook, plus illusion-completing pen. All the while he squinted at the magazine, trying to guess how many pages remained unread. The woman kept flicking backwards and forwards so, like her age, it was impossible to calculate. Returning his attention to his own section of table, Andrew inadvertently caught the eye of the librarian. This was something he tried not to do. She returned his stifled look of alarm with one of benign threat. He looked away, busying himself with not very much.

Most of the other regulars were settled now. He didn't know any of their names, which was part of the attraction of coming to the library rather than, say, the museum or bus station, where small talk would inevitably become an issue sooner or later. There was the man who smelled of cigarettes, the woman who smelled of something worse, and the youngish lad in the Big Issue tabard who looked perpetually surprised to be there. No sign of the mumsy-looking blonde woman, but she rarely appeared on a Monday. He scratched his beard, which seemed to be trying to suck all the hair from his head these days, and leaned forward on the desk to stop his belt from pulling.

His fingers began to tingle pleasantly as the central heating worked its way into his joints. Shooting a last jealous glance at his magazine, Andrew wandered through the dark wooden alcoves that surrounded the Reading Room and picked a book at random from the ceiling-high bank of shelves. It was historical, which was good, but something to do with Victorian Parliament, which wasn't exactly his cup of tea. He was more of a swords-and-sandals man. Still, the combined smells of old paper, dust and bulk-bought furniture polish began to work their usual spell on his mood, and the morning's mishaps faded. It was almost eleven before he knew it.

The comforting hush, the warmth and the literature began to lull him; the words swam on the pages and Andrew felt his head begin to nod. He shook it and rubbed his face. The woman with his magazine laughed, too loudly, drawing attention, so he bowed diligently over the Nuisance Removal Acts, hoping the librarian would not guess who the snort had been aimed at, or notice his doubtless red-rimmed eyes.

At half past eleven Andrew swapped his book for one on Norse mythology, which was much more to his taste, and slid his hand under the notebook to have a crafty nibble of his Kit Kat. He no longer minded that the woman still had his magazine. She seemed far more engrossed in the articles than he had been the day before, rocking backwards and forwards, following the words with fingers and lips. A studenty-looking couple were obviously finding this amusing; Andrew coughed just loud enough to ensure his glare was registered before returning to his own reading matter.

Now he had noticed her behaviour, however, it was difficult to un-notice it. He angled his chair a little, snapping his biscuit a centimetre at a time and sucking each piece until it could be swallowed silently. There was something fascinating in her fascination, he decided, something refreshing about a little liveliness in such a weary atmosphere. What he had initially assumed to be her lips following the text, he soon realised, was not quite true. She was repeating snippets to herself, only moving on when the next fact grabbed her. 'Forty-six per cent' became 'an angry mob' became 'Tooting Bec Lido', and so on. It was almost hypnotic, and Andrew realised that he had now become the one staring. He forced his attention back to Odin and chums, and left at four, as usual, to take the twenty-minute walk back to St Paul's.

The atmosphere in the hostel had lifted a little on his return as the beefier (and stroppier) participant of the morning's spat had decided to move out, to the relief of everyone else. Andrew spent the evening not thinking about Special Brew in front of the TV, but the woman in the library kept invading his consciousness. Whispered refrains layered themselves under the staccato sarcasm of reality show commentaries, wove their way through the understated awe of natural history programmes, as he half-dozed, half-read *The Evening Post*.

He was late again the next day, for no other reason than he was. The woman was there already, same spot, same magazine, same shopper by her feet. Although his seat in the window was free, he found himself returning to the position he had occupied the day before, enjoying the rhythm of her murmuring floating through the motes: 'democratic constitution'; 'brilliant pamphleteers'; 'unexpected uprising'.

By the eleven o'clock slump he had just about finished his book, and counteracted the drowsiness by wandering in and out of the gloomy cubby holes for a while, aware of how her voice sounded from the far corner of the room, the back of an alcove, the nook behind the stairs. Finally picking a biography of George Melly for a change, he decided to sit three seats nearer to her, moving his things along the desk as quietly as he could. He dared a smile, hoping for a glint of recognition, camaraderie even. But she angled her body away from him sharply as if he was trying to cheat at an exam. Andrew was left to sit with overly ebullient George for the rest of the day, wincing at the jazzman's satsuma-coloured tie, ultramarine hat, and other fashion eyesores. If it had not been for her continued mumbling he would have gone back to the hostel early, but instead he sat, not thinking about Tennent's Super, and prickling with embarrassment.

On Wednesday, after a listless night of unfocused angst and half-watched panel shows on Dave, a foggy-eyed Andrew marched straight past the receptionist and turned left, away from the earnest snoozery of the Reading Room. The Learning Centre was a bright, newish extension hiding at the end of the corridor, round what looked like a dead end. He rarely came here beyond browsing for a magazine now and then; after the dusty quiet, the laptops, workstations and abundance of public all came as a bit of a shock. He took a motoring monthly at random from the rack and settled himself in one of the low airport-style benches, feeling exposed without a desk, but resolved to wait a few days before returning to his usual spot.

It was difficult to concentrate. He found himself not thinking of Gold Label at fairly regular intervals as the clock turned with increasing sluggishness. It was difficult to snaffle any snacks out of his bag without being seen, and more people were giving him looks than they ever did round the corner. The old doubts began to surface again. How ridiculous it was, sitting here day after day when he could be out – in the cold – achieving something. Quite what he might achieve Andrew always found difficult to fathom, but today he wondered whether it would come to him if he just meandered round for long enough. He began to shuffle his belongings back into the carrier bag, barely aware of the person who came to sit next to him until the familiar undertone began.

'A brief but bloody battle fought on bleak moorland.'

Andrew resettled himself quickly, trying to make his packing-up look like a bit of general tidying. He tried another smile, enjoying the comforting aroma of inexpensive shower products she gave off this close, but the woman ignored him, studying the magazine which slid awkwardly on her lap. Andrew pretended to be absorbed by the motoring glossy, flicking as quickly as he could past pictures of Jeremy Clarkson and scowling at the inevitable gawpers. Hours passed, the clock's indifference coming close to outright cheek as his leg went to sleep and his bladder swelled.

At two o'clock she abruptly stood and swapped *Historical World* for *Wildlife Extra* from some box files stacked along the top of a bookcase. Though Andrew had not read a word of his petrolhead magazine, he waited a full ten minutes before recovering his long-lost reading matter. He doubted he would read a word of these articles either, but although the woman's attention to the resurgence of endangered Patagonian deer appeared steady, there seemed almost a chuckle at the heart of her 'synergistic conservation actions'.

By three, he felt in danger of rupturing something important, but managed to hold it in for another half an hour before the inevitable dash for the gents. That she had left by the time he got back did not come as much of a surprise.

He had group the next day, same as every Thursday, so Andrew didn't arrive at the library until gone eleven. He wondered where he would find her, if she was there at all, but her presence became apparent as he got to the top of the stairs. The woman was back in her usual space, with the nature magazine, repeating phrases noisily and taking deep wobbly breaths as she rocked. People were nudging, sitting further away from her than usual, so Andrew grunted loudly, grabbed the nearest book, and sat on the opposite side of the desk, one space along.

Geoff Boycott: A Cricketing Hero

Oh, bollocks. It was going to be a long day. He arranged his bits and bobs, acutely aware of the tremble in her voice, its slow, laborious return to normal. He thought about writing an apologetic note but that seemed, perversely, too weird, so he wondered instead if a smile was in order. He raised his head just as she lowered hers.

There was something different about her from this angle. The scrunchie had gone, and her hair was instead swept into some rolling curl thing down the back of her head. Her clothes looked different too: still mismatched (today a pink cardigan affair over a green flowery blouse), but they looked crisper somehow. A silver heart-shaped pendant dangled freely in front of her top button, and she smelled like the bubbly stuff his sister used to get given for Christmas by Aunt Janice. Fruity.

It was too confusing, so Andrew buried himself in biographical swagger. Every few minutes the muttering would stop and he would have the impression of being stared at, but by the time he looked up she was studying her magazine again.

'Shark attacks on humans are extremely rare, but should it ever happen, you need to know what to do.'

That's what it sounded like, anyway. He began to wonder what you should do. Swim fast? Play dead? Punch it on the nose? The surprised-looking Big Issue lad had a resonant fit of the hiccups, and everything got oddly syncopated. Andrew tapped his fingers on the desk along with the rhythm. The woman looked up, despite herself, and then looked down again far more quickly. Andrew hoped she had not taken his reaction the wrong way.

She looked … sort of beautiful. And also not. Andrew had become accustomed to her unkempt cleanliness, and had not expected to see the woman looking so, well, done up. Her complexion was brushed a pale cream, her eyes swept with smoky shadow. Cheeks and lips glowed softly.

Andrew would not in any way have considered himself an expert in feminine wiles but the idea of her applying all this stuff so – expertly – did not seem likely to him. She was sitting in silence, rocking, now, so he resumed his finger tattoo to try and reassure her, watching the strip of cheek visible to him mottle rosily beneath its dusting of powder.

She's said something to someone, he thought. Someone else thought this was a good idea. Sister? Carer? Andrew itched with the thought of being talked about. He itched for his companion's unease. Itched to be able to say something to her. His finger solo became heavier on the wooden desktop. The muted atmosphere of the library pushed down on him suddenly, the asphyxiating stink of pointless time-filling squeezing the breath from his lungs.

The woman jumped up. She dashed towards the exit, shopper knocking her calves. Andrew sat motionless, realising too late that he should have gone after her.

Story of my life, he thought bitterly.

Then he thought about getting utterly, utterly wankered. There was a Tesco Express just across College Green, but Andrew knew such a moment as this deserved marking by a proper session in a proper pub. He thought about The Bunch of Grapes, The Sedan Chair, even the airy anonymity of The Pitcher and Piano. The easy conversation of the lubricated, however things might end up.

Eleven forty-three. Wait till noon. Wait till noon, for God's sake.

Reasoning that it was a five minute walk to the harbourside bars, he packed his things away at eleven fifty-four, and was watching the second hand revolve on his watch face when the door to the Reading Room crashed open.

Andrew could not help but stare as she strode back towards him; the beauty that had been applied with such love was gone, scrubbed away by blue paper towels or loo roll or just a hearty splash from the basin. Her skin was damp and raw, her carefully twined hair pulled out into a wiry halo that dripped at the edges. She looked straight at him for the first time.

'CHRIST ON A BICYCLE,' she barked. Her eyes were as blue as George Melly's hat, and there was a Bristolian softness around the edge of her voice, even in her agitation, that he hadn't noticed before. Andrew opened his mouth to say something, then realised he had absolutely no clue what.

She held out her hand. 'Well don't just sit there like a cabbage, make yourself useful.'

'I ...'

She gestured again as she sat back down, and Andrew realised she was holding out a hairbrush: green, plastic, frizz-laden. He took it, circling to her side of the desk and drawing a chair from the next row to sit behind her. Remembering how his mother used to make his sister yell, he placed the flat of his free hand on top of the woman's head, inserting the bristles near the crown and pulling downwards. The brush seemed reluctant to obey, so he tugged a little harder.

'Oi,' she said sharply. Her fruity scent was overlaid with more than a hint of institutional soap now. Andrew laughed louder than he should have, forgetting about the luxury of a pint of Stella. He tried again, but the brush became more entangled, hanging unassisted when he let go in desperation. Now it was the woman's turn to giggle.

'You can't do that in here,' the librarian whispered by Andrew's head. 'You're disturbing people.'

'Sorry,' said Andrew. 'I was just ...'

'Look, I've got everyone else to consider. This isn't a hairdresser's salon. If you don't stop I'm afraid I'm going to have to ask you to leave.' The foundations of her sturdy voice trembled. 'It's just inappropriate behaviour in the library, isn't it?'

'It's not inappropriate,' said the woman, wrestling the hairbrush from her locks, 'we're not even touching, not really ...'

'I think that's for me ...'

'Not that it's any of your business ...'

'But ...'

'In fact, why don't you just piss off back to your desk and sit your fat arse down again?' She waved the hairbrush dangerously as she sprang to her feet, breath ragged, squaring up to her dumpy, M&S-clad adversary. Their antagonist paled; Andrew felt himself go pink. He looked at the two women, picked up his carrier bag, and picked up the hessian shopper.

'Yeah, piss off,' he said heartily. He gestured towards the exit. 'After you, miss.' He hoped the librarian would appreciate his mouthed apology as he followed his new friend out.

It was cold on Park Street. They almost huddled together as they made their way to the museum.

In the beginning there were chains. One hundred and eighty-six of them. Books were precious, so valuable that they had to be contained in the Library. Bristol's first free public library, opened in 1613 in Robert Redwood's Lodge in King Street, was a chained library.

I sit; gaze; wonder
at the myriad stories
ranged before my eyes.

Inside Story

Nicola Bennetts

'Feel free to touch.'

Frances enjoyed the look of puzzled delight when she invited visitors to sit in the armchairs, take the books from the shelves, read the magazines.

This room was different from the rest of the house. Here the tourists could time-travel a hundred years or more by stepping off the National Trust drugget. Here they could spend a short while as guests enjoying hospitality rather than day-trippers gawping at furniture and fittings.

'This was Lady Margaret's private sitting room,' she explained. The young couple looked incongruous in the chintzy surroundings, he in jeans (none too clean, Frances noticed) and T-shirt and the girl also in jeans with her T-shirt stretched across her bump. Six months at least, Frances supposed. So unbecoming. Why couldn't she cover her awkward shape with a nice little smock? But pregnancy was something to parade these days.

'We opened this room only last year,' she continued, 'when Lady Margaret died.'

'Did you know her?' the girl asked.

Yes, Frances was proud of her friendship with the old aristocrat. Of course there was a vast difference in age – Lady Margaret was ninety-six when she died – but Frances was flattered to have been treated as a social equal, given snippets of pre-war family gossip, and told about the tragic death of Margaret's fiancé.

The room was filling up now. Visitors were learning from each other, reading letters, leafing through the family photograph albums and putting records on the wind-up gramophone. Some of the volunteers had reservations about the touch-and-try approach but in Frances' experience it worked. People were thoughtful and handled things with care. She was glad the Trust had not gone as far as at Avebury Manor where children were allowed to bounce on the four-poster beds, but this personal sitting room brought the whole house and the family to life.

When she was on duty elsewhere Frances watched the tourists shuffle round morning room, drawing room, ballroom, paying polite homage to the portraits and porcelain but, if truth were told, heading for the gift shop and the tea-room. She could never decide which was worse, the bored who could be overheard muttering that one stately home was much like another, or the know-all who merely wanted to impress everyone by recognizing – in a loud voice – a piece of Chinese Chippendale or some Longton Hall china. Then – in the library where high shelves lined with leather-bound tomes reduced most people to hushed respect – you could guarantee that some wag would ask, 'Do you think anyone has ever read any of these books?'

No one would pose that question in Lady Margaret's sunny sitting room where the books lining the walls spoke of reading for pleasure, their spines a kaleidoscope of colours and their pages worn with turning. Frances had been part of the team preparing the room before it was opened to the public. They had examined every book, checking the inscriptions, gently shaking the pages and finding within them envelopes, lists, several dance cards, some tiny sketches and, in one, a ten-shilling note.

She was pleased to see someone looking at the shelf of children's books: *Alice, The Just So Stories, Little Women* – all the favourite classics. The woman, smiling as if she was revisiting her own childhood, was different from the usual National Trust visitor. No anorak or stout shoes, no jeans or T-shirt, she was smartly dressed with a sharp yellow scarf looped over a black skirt and jacket, leather knee boots and an expensive shoulder bag. She might have been going to a business meeting or a speaking engagement. She wore a wedding ring and a very large solitaire diamond so, Frances deduced, she must be married – or had been, for there was no sign of any companion and the room had suddenly emptied of other people.

'I heard you say you knew Lady Margaret,' said the woman. Thirty or thirty-five, Frances decided. Perhaps she was one of those television historians, looking for a subject for her next series. Did she recognise her? Perhaps, though she couldn't name her.

'Yes,' Frances said. 'I got to know her very well over the last ten years. A remarkable woman.'

'She never married?'

'No, her fiancé was killed right at the start of the war. He was awarded a posthumous Victoria Cross. He was just twenty-five when he died; Lady Margaret was twenty-one.'

'Would you say his death affected Lady Margaret? Was that why she never married? Was she bitter or depressed?'

What extraordinary questions. Who wouldn't be affected by the death of a fiancé? Frances wasn't certain she wanted some television psycho-documentary made about her friend. 'She was heartbroken when George died, and there was never anyone who could take his place, but she wasn't bitter. She was immensely proud of his bravery, his service to his country,' Frances said.

'But immediately after his death, might she have been a little unbalanced for a while, do you think?' the young woman asked.

This was becoming impertinent. Frances decided she must put an end to the inquisition. 'No, but I'm afraid I don't feel it's proper for me to discuss such matters when her ladyship is dead.'

'I'm sorry. I shouldn't have asked. I just wanted so much to get an understanding of her. This room is very warm and welcoming, the books are those of an intelligent, interesting woman. It's hard not to like her.'

'She was very likable,' Frances said. 'She was quite formidable on first meeting, but she was down-to-earth, and she had a great sense of humour.'

The young woman moved to one of the arm chairs and sat down. 'I ought to explain. I already know a little bit about her. My grandmother worked here. She was a parlour maid.'

'I see.' Frances was suddenly uneasy. 'How long ago was that?'

'She left in 1940. It was just after the family had received news of the death of Lady Margaret's fiancé. My grandmother was dismissed and sent packing without a reference.'

Frances stiffened. Don't say the grandmother had been pregnant. The old Earl, Lady Margaret's father, had been notorious. Was this young woman going to claim some kind of kinship with the family? Had she had a DNA test which would prove her case? She struggled to keep her voice steady. 'There must have been some reason for her dismissal.'

'Oh, yes. She was accused of theft.'

'Reason enough,' Frances said.

'She was accused of theft, but I'm certain she was innocent. What really devastated her was the fact that Lady Margaret didn't believe her. She never got over that.'

'But there must have been some grounds for thinking she was guilty,' Frances said.

'Pretty shaky grounds, if you ask me. There was a ten-shilling note which Lady Margaret swore she'd left on a table in this very room, and it was missing. My grandmother was the only other person to have been in here. She was certain there was no money on the table but how could she prove it? It was her word against Lady Margaret's and that was that. Ten shillings. That's fifty pence, isn't it?'

A ten-shilling note. Frances thought back to the inspection of the books before the room was opened – and the ten-shilling note they'd found.

So? It didn't prove anything. Just a coincidence. There was no need to complicate matters by mentioning it. 'Ten shillings was a lot of money before the war,' she said.

'Yes, and my grandmother was poor. She knew what ten shillings would buy, but that didn't mean she stole it. She'd worked here for two years; they should have known they could believe her.'

The old parlour maid must be in her nineties by now; what did she expect to gain by her granddaughter's visit? Come to that, just what was the granddaughter's game? It was unhealthy – obsessive – to be pursuing the matter after so many years. She needed to steer the conversation to safer ground. 'Does your grandmother live locally?'

'She did. She died two weeks ago. That's why I'm here; it was her funeral yesterday.'

Frances murmured awkward condolences as the young woman continued. 'I thought I'd stay overnight and visit The House – that's what she always called it. I wanted to see where she'd worked, get a feel of the place.'

Frances relaxed. The grandmother was dead, the granddaughter obviously lived some distance away. This was the last she would see of her. Perhaps it wouldn't hurt to tell her what they had found in the books. Allow closure – that was what people were after these days, wasn't it?

'I don't think my grandmother would approve of my telling you all this.'

Then I wish you wouldn't, thought Frances. And neither, she decided, would Lady Margaret approve of her gossiping about a ten-shilling note which just happened to be in one of the books. It would be a betrayal of trust.

'Let bygones be bygones – that was her philosophy,' the young woman continued. 'In a way the war helped because she could get a job despite having no reference.'

Really the young woman was unstoppable. Where were all the other visitors? Tucking into carrot and coriander soup, quiche and salad, she supposed, taking a quick look at her watch.

'What did she do?' Clearly, Frances realised, she was in for the whole story. She might as well try to sound interested.

'She worked in a munitions factory, but it wasn't the same. She'd been so proud of working here and she really cared about the family.'

So proud of working here. It was hard not to like the little parlour maid, to feel sorry for her plight. And the granddaughter was quite touching even if she talked too much. Perhaps …

'Oh what a charming room.' An American accent – four women all wearing luminous orange stickers on their lapels stood in the doorway. A coach tour, thought Frances, as more visitors each sporting an orange label appeared. Rescue. No need to say any more.

The granddaughter stood up and smiled at Frances, 'It's been nice to meet you and tell you my grandmother's story. Thank you for your interest. Goodbye.'

I wasn't interested, thought Frances, managing to smile as she said goodbye. The young woman hovered outside the door studying the portraits in the corridor. Well, she'd move to another room soon enough.

Frances turned to talk to the orange-sticker brigade. 'This was Lady Margaret's private sitting room and we want you to make yourselves at home here. You're welcome to read the books and magazines, and to play records on the gramophone – though you'll have to wind it up first.'

Laughter, and the visitors began to explore. Questions, and nods of interest as she told them about Lady Margaret's determination to remain in the house; how almost to the end she might be seen in the garden dead-heading her roses, and how much it had amused her when visitors assumed she was an employee or a National Trust volunteer.

'What you call a character, I suppose,' said one of the women, 'but quite steely.'

'Oh no, I like her,' said another, examining the books. 'She sounds real gutsy. And I guess this room could tell some stories. Romance, honour, chivalry.'

'In here, maybe, but what about the servants' lives? Hard work, low pay, they were no better than possessions.'

'Different times, different ways.'

'Give me today's ways. All right for Lady Margaret but just suppose you'd been her servant.'

They were no better than possessions. Frances shuddered as she listened to the banter. *Just suppose you'd been her servant.*

She went to the door. There was just a chance, and – yes – the young woman was there, not far down the corridor, still examining the portraits.

'Excuse me!' Frances called. 'There's something I should have mentioned ...'

In the eighteenth century Redwood Lodge was demolished and for £1,301/8/1 an elegant new library was built. The chains were removed from the books. As well as the good folk of Bristol, Sir Humphrey Davy, Samuel Taylor Coleridge and Robert Southey borrowed from the library.

A stranger's bookshelves:
obscure illumination
of a life unknown.

How Old Dreams Are Read

Shirley Wright

'*Before your eyes, the skull will glow and give off heat. Trace that light with your fingertips. That is how old dreams are read.*'
Hard-boiled Wonderland and the End of the World, Haruki Murakami.

The light was fierce and burned my eyes. Cautiously I placed a hand either side of the skull, reaching along the threads of memory. Dry beneath my touch, it began to pulse and murmur. But the words had no meaning. They spoke a language of lost time, singing of dreams beyond imagination.

'I cannot do this,' I said to the Librarian. 'I cannot read the dreams.'

He smiled. 'Patience is needed. Old dreams have travelled far and your journey may be long.'

'Why do the unicorns die?' I asked, sick of the babble in my head.

'They die and are reborn. Thus is the well-spring of memory refreshed, while we reap the harvest of the dead.' He pointed to the rows of unicorn skulls that lined the shelves on the Library walls.

It was late. Tired and hungry, I collected my things and went home. Eating supper by the kitchen window, I watched foals playing outside in the moonlight. Their long silver horns dipped and swayed as they pranced, and all the world seemed white. Winter was coming. In the freezing snow, many unicorns would die.

Before I fell asleep I resolved to find my shadow. Together we would discover a place of safety for these creatures, far from our cold lands, a place where my shadow and I might become one. The skull would lead me there; for some reason I felt sure of this and I knew what I must do.

Next day at dawn I jumped out of bed and dressed quickly, impelled by a sense of urgency. After a hurried breakfast I ran to the Watchtower to speak with the Guardian.

'What brings you here so early?' he asked, surprised to see me.

But I found I had no answer. Picking up an axe, I helped him chop wood for the brazier before heading into town. Fires were being lit on every street corner, small suns in the grey morning. From time to time sparks flew and fizzed on the icy cobbles. I observed their trajectory, the way they arced and spat, the paths they followed.

The Professor would be expecting me, pacing the corridors with my test results clenched in his fist, ready to berate me. However, I knew of another way in via my uncle's workshop, the old door concealed behind mounds of straw. At this hour Uncle would be out feeding the herd, so I made directly for the barn. Scrambling under his workbench, I pushed the huge bales aside to reveal the entrance and slipped through. Once inside I ran quickly up the stairs, taking the marbled walk that led away from the classrooms towards the Library. Last night I had kept the key and now I slipped it from my pocket, though nervousness made me fumble the lock.

Unicorn skulls sat on every surface like a chorus of the dead. Cold air swept over me. On the highest shelf, next to a crumbling specimen from days when dreams came true, I spotted the skull I had tried to read yesterday, the one to which I felt drawn. I recognised it immediately. Or perhaps it recognised me. A few steps up the ladder and it was in my hands, then tucked away under my cloak where it nestled invisible in the crook of my arm.

'The Professor is looking for you,' said the Librarian as he walked in. A dusting of frost silvered his hair. 'Your studies must take precedence, young man.' He smiled. 'I know how you struggle. Come back tonight and together we will try again to read what is written.'

I nodded, not trusting my tongue. As I scurried away through the atrium, a look of surprise crossed his face. 'Wait … come back! You cannot take …'

But I was gone. Through the black curtains, down the steps, out into the barn. Replacing the straw as best I could, I ran on to the street and turned sharp right to where traders queued for the gate, blowing on their fingers and stamping up and down to keep from freezing. Their wagons were full to overflowing.

'Hey! What do you think you're …?' It was a tradesman I knew, and he winked as I hopped on to his cart and yanked the tarpaulin over my head. 'One of these days, my lad …' he muttered, then promptly forgot me as he pumped his feet in tune to a tirade against life. 'Buggering guards. Freezing my balls off here and not a sodding Watcher ready to …'

I crouched low. Warm against my left side, the skull pulsed a welcome between my racing heartbeats. Almost I thought I could hear a voice.

Thus far I had acted upon instinct, inventing my adventure as opportunity presented itself. My shadow once told me that every act brings consequences, though my promotion to Assistant Librarian had no obvious cause. Simply I was there, and the Librarian had thrust a date stamp into my hand. In this ordinary way I had gained access to knowledge. Would the Professor raise the alarm at my absence or give up waiting for me and return to marking papers? Temporal theory was such a difficult subject, obscure and unfriendly towards a daydreaming boy.

With a jolt, we were off. Wheels rumbled beneath me, juddering my spine and rattling my teeth. My friend shouted obscenities as we crossed the gateway, then settled to a contented whistle. While he urged the horses uphill, I resolved to make a plan.

Once confident we had cleared the Watchtower's reach, I wriggled my head out to breathe crisp air. Not far from here, the path would veer off into woodland. My destination lay the other way, down into the Valley of the Sun. Although the sky today was more overcast than usual and sunlight seemed an impossibility, I recalled the place of our last meeting. Recalled it clearly, with the intensity of an old truth. The place where I had last encountered my shadow.

As the cart swung westward, I leapt from the back and tumbled into bushes at the roadside. The skull, safe inside my cloak, bumped against my chest. Where the horn had been removed, rough bone scratched my skin.

The clip-clop of hooves soon faded. Gathering my cloak around me, I ran half-crouching towards the edge of a deep ravine that gashed our world as though some drunken giant had wielded a carving knife. Hanging over the edge of the precipice, feet hooked through tree roots, I peered straight down. From far, far away, as if from underground, came river sounds and the promise of sunlight on sparkling water.

I came here years ago with my parents. There had been summers then and days spent in the countryside. The last of the Watchtowers was being built and Guardians were queuing up for work, large men with small brains, eager to help and believing that safety lay behind walls. I thought I could remember the exact spot – rough grass beside a fast-flowing river and sharp rocks like needles tipping the sky. Several unicorns had been grazing by the water's edge. Mother had called out 'Look! Look!' in her high, excited voice. The sun's angle was such that when I spun round, my shadow, which lay dark across the field, had seemed to stretch far into the distance, as though taking the lead and inviting me to follow. 'Run,' Father shouted, 'run,' and I was eager to play the game. But the faster I ran the more my shadow outstripped me. I chased and chased after it but finally I lost it altogether. When I retraced my steps to our picnic blanket I found their bodies, black with blood.

Since then I have lived behind the walls and time has slowed. I realise now I have no idea of my age nor how long ago it was that my parents died. Sometimes I feel a thousand years old, though the Professor would tell you I am a thoughtless boy.

The descent over the cliff edge was steep. 'Yesterday is the hardest road to follow,' the Librarian had told me. 'It is a path of snares and footfalls, set about with thorns that snag and potholes that will trip you up. But it is the only route forward. This is the paradox of being.' I was slipping and sliding now, terrified at any moment I would twist an ankle or, worse still, smash the skull which had started to drum a rhythm against my ribcage. Did it know my plan and approve?

Bouncing from tree to boulder I crashed through the dense undergrowth, ripping my clothes on branches that snapped as I flew past. Down and down I slithered, desperately holding tight to the skull for fear of losing it. Then a sudden slick of mud and my feet went from under me, plunging me to the bottom in a tumbling blur. For a few seconds I was too dazed to move, but from the corner of one eye I became aware of a light shining, soft and milky in the distance. I realised that my arms were empty, my cloak was flapping open on the grass, and a dull pain was beating in my head. When I reached up to probe my forehead, my hand encountered wetness. I must have hurt myself, though I quickly scrambled to my feet so it was nothing serious. Some yards away, thrown from my grasp, lay the unicorn skull, intact like me and glowing as if lit from within.

'Before your eyes, the skull will glow and give off heat. Trace that light with your fingertips. That is how old dreams are read.' The

Librarian always counselled patience. 'When the moment is ready. When *you* are ready for lost words.'

A fast-flowing river. A shaft of sunlight and a presence by my side.

I picked the skull up and held it firmly between my hands. Warmth, like the promise of a memory, washed over me and, reaching my fingers along the great bone, I closed my eyes.

When I open them I am deep within the rock face, groping my way through a narrow passage full of such twists and turns it is soon impossible to tell forwards from backwards. The air reeks and everywhere the sound of dripping water. At my feet, stones and potholes and slime; above my head, jagged rock that threatens to gash my brains out. Cradled in my outstretched hands the skull pulses, growing brighter the further I move through the tunnel. But it is also inside my head, behind my eyes, seeing the path forward and urging me on. I walk cautiously but with new resolve through a darkness that cleaves before me, yielding like the gorge itself to the flow of time.

I emerge into daylight. A swathe of green greets me. Blinking hard, my eyes accustom to the glare and then I stumble, astonished. Huge stone buildings surround this green place and people, some on foot, some on two-wheeled contraptions, hurry by in carnival clothes the like of which I have never seen before. Such a riot of colour. A woman with purple and orange hair; a man in red trousers conversing with another who sucks upon a white stick that glows fire. Smoke curls from his puckered lips. They bustle past me, unsurprised by a tonsured boy in rags. About to follow them I am startled by a sudden but familiar rending of the air and I spin round to the peal of bells; at my back the bulk of an ancient church. Opposite this, on the other side of the green, a long and endless building sweeps past silver glints of water. A building which curves, which is pink! And everywhere a low rumble that seems to buzz through my teeth, and shining carriages in blue and grey and black and yellow rolling along with not a horse in sight. They move as if propelled by magic.

A boy about my age bumps into me. He seems distracted, chattering into the palm of his own hand. 'Sorry, what? Yeah, text you later. Just nipping into the library.' Then he bounds two at a time up a nearby flight of steps and into the stone edifice on my left, still talking to himself. Or rather, to his hand. Perhaps his mind is enfeebled. From the door he has left open two women exit, animated and giggling. Their short garments astonish me, and their loud voices.

I feel excited and start to tremble. I realise I have no idea where I am or who these people might be. Hiding the skull deep inside my cloak, I decide to enter the old building and find out. It may hold the answer to my questions. Then something catches my eye; a dark shape, an outline on the ground in front of me, going where I go. As we move forward together, I glance up at the wide arc of the pink palace opposite, at the reach of its sweeping roof.

I look. And I stare and stare.

Perched high, as if surveying the city, two golden unicorns stand guard over this strange new world.

By the twentieth century the King Street Library was too small. On College Green, the Old Deanery and Canons House were demolished to make way for a new building. The London firm of H. Percy Adams beat sixty other entrants to win the competition for the best design for the library.

So many lives lived,
so many loves lost and found
here, on every shelf.

The Library At Alexandria

Nina Milton

'So that's the core point of my research,' said Emmitt. 'Did the library at Alexandria ever really burn down?'

'Burn down?' said Ashley. 'What, arson?'

'Of course not *arson*. This is fourth century BCE. Idiots didn't go round with cans of petrol in those days.' Or did they, he wondered. How did he know that some random serf with a grudge might not want to set a blaze going, for the sake of watching something he'd never understand burn to the ground? 'We're talking about a wonder of the world here; the great library that contained all knowledge and learning in ancient times.'

'I guess it could have been accidental. I mean … books burn fast, don't they?'

'They didn't have books. It wasn't books at all.'

'A library? Without books?'

Emmitt shook his head. He felt his hair shift as his neck jerked back and forth. Before meeting Ashley for this date, he'd promised himself two things: a visit to the barbers, and to *not* get over-passionate about the library at Alexandria. A haircut had been forfeit to finishing a first full draft of his thesis, and within the time it had taken to order the meal, here he was, practically rising from his seat with emotion. Talk to *her*, he told himself. The girl you're taking out. Ask her about herself.

'Have you ever been to Alexandria?'

'I wouldn't have thought so, Emmitt. I don't even know where it is.'

They were served with a starter of hand-dived scallops on a seaweed bed. Emmitt had chosen the food because Ashley had been staring at the menu with a panicked look in her eye, but if he was honest, he wasn't all that used to the fine dining experience himself. He was trying to look more at home than Ashley, nodding to the waiter that the wine was not corked, and choosing from the menu with confidence. After all, he'd picked Bell's Diner because he'd wanted to impress her. But now she was staring down at the uneaten scallops and turning the amber ring on her right hand round and round. She had such a neat frame, the bodice of her dress clung to it, showing her ribs through the printed cotton. Maybe she only ate diet food.

It was inconceivable that his search for Hypatia would fail because he'd taken his date to the wrong restaurant.

In portraits, Hypatia wore her hair swept up, encircled with thin bands. She held her chin slightly down as if in contemplation. Seated on marble, inside the library at Alexandria, she'd have students at her feet, and their chins would be raised, their eyes trained on her calm face. Emmitt knew her voice would be like a clear note on a flute, not too high and never raised in exasperation at a student's foolishness. There were tiny lines at either side of her eyes, because she smiled whenever she could, but he didn't imagine her laughing out loud, not a big, rollicking laugh. Her thoughts were too controlled for outright merriment – she was chief librarian, after all. Men came from all over the world to hear her speak. Not for her beauty or the elegance of her carriage, but because she held the secrets of mathematics, philosophy and astronomy. All those years ago, her voice raised and fluting, dressed in flowing white, she lectured on geometry and number theory, on the tables of stars and planets and the philosophies of Plato. She held tight to a world that was slipping away.

From the moment Emmitt had seen Ashley on Queen's Road, bouncing towards him on stilt-tall heels, he had wanted her to be his Hypatia. The black shine of her eyes, rimmed with kohl, caught his attention. She had thighs that almost concaved under the pressure of her skinny Levis, while her top half was obscured by a sort of floaty, swirly thing in tribal colours. Her black hair was piled on top of her head, encircled with a thin plastic band.

Emmitt had turned as she'd passed by and followed her as she'd swerved up the steps of the Students' Union. He'd winkled her out from her shell of friends and bought her a rum and coke. She'd giggled at his name, but wouldn't say why, insisting she hated her own. 'Good,' he'd said, without meaning to. It was too early to explain that she would have to change her name.

He would take a white pashmina and drape it over her dark hair and once round her neck and utter three times: Hypatia, Hypatia, Hypatia. She would be his muse made flesh.

Ashley laid her cutlery over her starter to signify she'd done with it. She'd barely nibbled the edge of a scallop and pushed the seaweed to one side. He struggled not to tell her that her starter alone had cost him a tenner of the scholarship money he had to survive on. He nudged his own plate away. Watching Ashley play with the scallops had robbed him of his usual relish.

'Egypt,' he said, and coughed on a morsel of food.

'What?'

'Egypt. Is where Alexandria is.'

'Yeah? I've been to Egypt and I've never heard of it.'

'That's because it's nowhere near Sharm El Sheikh.' He hadn't meant to sound waspish, but he was terrified that she might turn out to be dim. She'd had a bag full of books on her shoulder when he'd seen her on Queen's Road; surely that meant some semblance of intellect? Over the rum and coke, he'd asked her what she was studying.

'Life, Emmitt. Yeah. Life. In all its suffering and remorse.'

'Philosophy?'

'Yeah. You could say that.' She'd laughed, showing teeth white as stone. As temple stone.

All the time he sat with her, she hadn't touched her drink. Mostly, she'd looked at the door to the bar, at the people who came and went. She didn't initiate any of their conversation, but surely that wouldn't matter. Emmitt was happy to talk for them both. Now, she was quietly watching the world go by on the street outside, and her pose had Grecian qualities. When she smiled, there were wrinkles around her eyes. Although they might have to work on her voice, soften the tones. And get rid of that giggle.

The waiter swooped in and rescued both dishes, sliding a little more wine into each of their glasses. The bottle was almost done, but anyway Emmitt had ordered a Saint Emillion to go with the wood pigeon and chanterelles. He swallowed his half glass and the waiter took the hint and refilled it, leaving a centimetre at the bottom of the bottle. He could feel the alcohol swimming in his head and he was grateful. As soon as the waiter had turned his back, he sloshed the final dregs into his glass.

'The interesting thing is,' he began, 'that it's just possible the entire burning thing is a myth. OK. It is said that Caesar set fire to the harbour when he tried to capture Pompey at Alexandria, and legend has it that the flames ravaged the city, talking the library down. But there's no record of that happening. Then there's the story of Theopilus.'

'Weird name.'

'Well, it's Latin.'

'But he lived in Egypt.' She frowned, as if she was trying to keep up.

'Well, yes, he was Patriarch of the city. Would you believe he is the patron saint of arsonists? It's possible he destroyed all the scrolls when he was converted to Christianity. Early Christians weren't keen on any knowledge outside their own.'

'Scrolls!' She giggled as if it was comic. 'D'you know, it does ring a bell, Alexandria. But that's probably because my friend's called Alex.'

'It was named for its founder, Alexander, but all this happened hundreds of years after he died.' It was clear she had no idea who bloody Alexander was, but Emmitt didn't stop. He was into his theme now, and he would set it down. It was good to be able to do this – sum up in a few words, in the time it took to eat a meal. It would surely help when he got his Viva.

'See, I don't think Theopilus destroyed the library,' he said, 'because it's still standing in 500 AD when the area's rife with trouble. Muslims, Jews, Christians and Pagans, all trying to win supremacy in this prosperous city, fighting for it. To the death. It's a crossroads, you see. Close to borders. Important. More like a small kingdom with no one laying down the law. Each sect hating the other. After dark, they would grab members of any other religion and drag them through the streets, or corner and slay them.'

'Sounds like nowadays.'

Their main course arrived, the pigeon glazed in its rich sauce and the vegetables artfully arranged. Emmitt spent a few moments taking in the aroma, but his mind was in Alexandria; he lived in it, and loved in it too. It was why he had followed Ashley into the Students' Union.

'I don't believe the library was ever completely lost. That's the basis of my study. There are too many stories, and they all protest too much.'

He waited. She should ask something. *Never lost? Whatever*

d'you mean? But Ashley was already tucking in, slicing and chewing the meat.

For seven hundred years, the library was a thing of wonder, but it was only a small part of a spectacular museum so vast it had its own zoo and shaded gardens, and walkways leading out into the city and even to the palace of Alexandria. In his mind, Emmitt could take an entire hour to walk through the museum, up the wide staircases through pillared storey upon pillared storey. He'd linger in the circular domed hall which rose above the city, and take in the observatory tower where scholars used to gaze at the stars. But he'd always end up in the library, where the papyrus scrolls, neatly scribed in ancient Linear B, were hoarded; stories of the peoples across the fertile lands. Sumer and Phoenicia, Babylon, Assyria, Egypt and Greece and Rome. At the heart of this was Hypatia, the Neo-Platonist who studied the pagan principles of science and logic. A giant of a woman lost in history's misogyny.

'Emmitt?' Ashley was saying softly. 'Eat your dinner.'

He looked down. He hadn't yet tasted a morsel.

'Weird thing to serve,' she said. 'Chicken and crisps.'

'Game chips,' he corrected. He stuffed some mushroom and a sliver of meat into his mouth and talked through it, his voice raised. 'And pigeon.'

'What?' She sat back in her chair.

'Pigeon.'

'Pigeon! I haven't been eating some lousy pigeon, have I?'

'It's game, *Ashley*.' Call her Ashley, he told himself. Constant reminder of a bad mistake. 'A discerning taste. Hung for its flavour.'

'Come on. There's bleeding pigeons flying all over Bristol. You wouldn't have to be very discerning to shoot a few.' She drove her fork through the miniature leg, already gnawed to its bone, and hoisted it up, twisting it slightly to examine it from all sides. 'Millions of them strutting about the Centre, yet we get these titchy portions.'

'This is fine dining.'

'It's not *fine* to eat pigeon.'

'We should aspire to fine things,' said Emmitt, but there was a tinge of despair in his voice, he could hear it himself. She wasn't doing a degree, that was plain. She didn't have a great mind. And when he looked at her hair more closely, it didn't look Greek at all. Just roughed up and pinned into a bunch.

The library had been the city's instrument of power through knowledge, dedicated to the nine Muses. The Alexandrians loved the Muses above all the goddesses, because they drew down inspiration in both the arts and the sciences, and had been brought into life to help poor mortals forget evil and sorrow. But Hypatia's Alexandria did not forget sorrow; it fostered evil. It had become a violent city, split into volatile factions which abhorred each other's beliefs. Muslim against Jew. Jew against Christian. And they all hated the Pagans, with their ancient understanding of atoms and stellar precession.

Gangs from the factions were at each other's throat every night, wax torches illuminating marching columns of yelled hatred. The Muslims went for the Jews and the Jews fought back. The Christians, believing this world was theirs now their religion had taken hold, took issue with Jews and Muslims alike, but when Christians were slain in number their retaliation was almost always against the Pagans. Their old gods seemed the easiest to defeat – almost dead anyhow. One dark Alexandrian night, the beautiful, clever Hypatia was dragged into the streets and knifed down. She still clung to the teachings of the Greek philosophers who believed the earth might be round and that many gods ruled in a different heaven. By the fourth century, all this felt like archaic heresy. Hypatia had become an anachronism in this world of fundamental belief, and when she was slaughtered, her learning and philosophy perished with her. But perhaps, just perhaps, the library didn't suffer the same fate. With the right research grant, it might be possible to locate one of the library buildings, hidden still, perhaps, under the modern city.

'I'm longing to go to Alexandria. I can't wait to see it for myself.'

'You haven't been there? Egypt's quite cheap on the plane.'

'I have no intention of going with some package tour,' said Emmitt. 'I want to be able to wander around the ruins of the ancient city for as long as I need and with no one directing me. You can still see the citadel and the Roman theatre.'

Ashley was staring at him as if nothing he said made sense to her. She didn't possess a soul that would allow her to understand. On Queen's Road she'd been a black-eyed mystery, slender as the stem of a glass. But here, in the restaurant, she hardly knew what she was eating. She was nothing, a mirage of the past. He wanted this date to be over so that he might never see her again. He'd been a fool to think he would find his lady of Alexandria on a Bristol street.

'You should do it. Just use your student loan. Do it!'

'I could take you there,' he found himself saying. 'I'll take you there and show you Pompey's Pillar. Teach you about such things.' Emmitt laughed, once. 'You would understand, if I showed you.'

'I do understand,' said Ashley. 'I can see it stirs you up. You look all excited and upset at the same time.'

She had that way with her, he had to admit. She was sad when others were sad. This chap had come into the Students' Union while they were there. Actually, he'd glanced over at them, but quickly looked away. He'd taken a drink to a high stool in the window, his shoulders slouched as he walked, as if he'd had a bad day. And when Emmitt looked back at Ashley, he saw that she'd begun to weep sympathetic tears, as if she'd seen into his mind.

He gestured to the waiter. The plates, still loaded with food, might as well go. 'D'you want a dessert?'

She shrugged. 'My mum would tell me I couldn't have one, if I hadn't eaten my dinner.'

'Mine was the same. Couldn't afford to be soft about food.'

'I didn't get to know my dad, so my mum had to manage on her own.'

'Was she divorced, your mum, like mine?'

'What? Nah. Never married in the first place.'

'I won't ever do that. Ever.'

'Get married?'

'Walk out on my kid.'

'Ain't fair, is it?'

'Anyway, I'm basing my doctorate on that hypothesis – the library did not burn down. I'm discussing the lack of primary evidence conclusively proving that its contents were burnt.'

She opened her arms in a Gallic shrug. 'Why would anyone do that anyhow? Destroy something so beautiful and meaningful as all the knowledge in the world?'

'People are always doing it, aren't they? Because they fear what they don't understand.'

Her eyes had grown very round. They verged on blackness at the centres, like a place to step, so that your toes gripped the edge of a dark lake. He gave his shoulders a shake. 'I mean, we know some scrolls survived, so how can we be sure that other copies didn't? It's my belief that they're hidden somewhere.'

'Wow,' said Ashley. 'That would be great, wouldn't it? To find them?'

He nodded. It would be great. After all, the Dead Sea Scrolls survived from around the same time, discovered in earthenware jars inside a cave. 'There were thousands of scrolls,' he said. 'Hundreds of thousands. Why, Mark Anthony gave Cleopatra over two hundred thousand scrolls for the library alone. They might still be somewhere.'

The waiter was hovering. She'd been right; the portions were small. He craved something sweet, to fill the ache inside him. 'I'll have the rhubarb, almond and blood orange Crème Fraîche, please.' He opened his mouth to continue, then closed it again. 'What would you like, Ashley?'

'The gingerbread thing, please.' She passed the sweet menu to the waiter and leaned over the table. 'Hey, Emmitt, the penny's dropped now. I *have* heard of Alexandria. It's where they invented the Tarot.'

Emmitt was still smarting from the casual way she'd ordered the gingerbread soufflé. 'Sorry?'

'Come on. Doing all this research, you must know the story.'

Emmitt could feel his brow creasing, his eyes narrowing. She dipped down and snatched her bag from under her chair.

'Look, like this.' She opened the bag and pulled out a small cardboard box, glossy and garish. It hit the table with a thump. 'Tarot,' she said, lifting the lid.

She spread her napkin across the table to save the cards from spills. She formed a fan of four or five of them. 'The Greater Arcana. That's supposed to be where it came from. The library at Alexandria. Only, I never realised it was in bleeding Egypt. Might have gone and had a look, if I'd known.'

'I don't believe,' Emmitt began, 'that the great scrolls of knowledge in the Alex …'

'But yeah, Emmitt. That's the point. Not *knowledge* so much – not, like, *facts* and things. It was wise things they needed to save. They drew it on to twenty-two cards. The story of man- and womankind. Get me?'

'No,' said Emmitt.

'Deep wisdom. You know, arcane and secretly kept.'

'Sophia,' said Emmitt, suddenly. 'Greek for wisdom. And she was a goddess, honoured by the Alexandrians.' By Hypatia, in fact. He blinked, and Ashley pushed the cards towards him.

'See this one? The chariot? That tells you of victory and of will. And assertion of yourself. Achieving things, too. Holding on to your anger and assuming the reins of power.'

'You learned all that,' Emmitt accused, 'by rote, perhaps.'

'Yeah, but you don't learn what lies beneath. You can't learn that. Once you lay the cards down, and let them seep into your mind. What they tell you then. That comes from elsewhere.'

He could picture the bag, over her shoulder, on Queen's Road. It hadn't been crammed with books after all, but with packs of cards. He tossed the rest of the red down his throat. His head was floating, he was sinking.

The waiter hovered, two desserts on his tray. Emmitt whispered across the table. 'Clear your place.'

In seconds, she had bundled her pack away and the napkin was back on her lap. But as Emmitt watched, he became aware of her willow-deft brown fingers with their straight-cut nails, the strength behind every movement. He looked at her chocolate-brown eyes again, and the cheap hoop earrings he'd hated when she'd first walked into the restaurant. It all slotted into place. An understanding transformed him.

She's got ancient blood, he thought. For thousands of years her family travelled, north from the southern lands. People who crossed palms with silver.

In front of him was his dessert. A chopped fruit salad with nuts and plain yogurt, which had cost him as much as a freezerful of supermarket puds. And Ashley had exactly what she'd ordered, a gingerbread thing. 'Just like my mum used to make,' she said, spooning it into her mouth. 'When I'd eaten my dinner, at least.' She winked at him.

He looked at her through his empty wine glass. He couldn't speak for a moment. He was caught up with things that were beautiful and meaningful and easily destroyed.

'You came from Egypt,' he told her. 'Generations ago. Millennia ago. You came from the land of the lotus. I know you did. You are Hypatia herself.'

Ashley finished her mouthful of soufflé and took a clearing sip of her leftover wine. Then she spoke.

'Hypatia? Who the hell is Hypatia?'

Cathedral, Abbey Gatehouse, Library – old and new were harmoniously linked by the design for the twentieth-century building. The designer at H Percy Adams was Charles Holden, just twenty-seven years old and at the start of a hugely successful career, but a modest and self-effacing man who in later years twice refused a knighthood.

Secret history.
If I take the time to search,
all will be revealed.

The Dis-associate

Louise Gethin

At the age of twelve, I was given to taking solitary walks across the Downs and into the woods beyond. Although I had family and friends, I suffered what can only be described as an emptiness of spirit alongside a fragmentation of self. While I appeared whole on the outside, each fragment inside pulled in a different direction, like a mirror shattering over and over, reflecting me in splinters. I felt this most acutely when I stood on a ledge at the end of the line of trees overlooking the Avon Gorge and watched the brown ribbon of water flow below. A desire to lean forward and embrace the force of gravity surfaced at these times, although I always pulled back.

I sought solace in books.

Henleaze Library was a small unassuming brick building nestled next to what was the Cock O'The North pub. I discovered it through a school friend. The first time, like a tour guide, she acted as a portal to an unknown city.

Once I had my own library card, I crept in there and, undisturbed, relished titles, ran my fingers over spines of novels, opened them, dipped in, dipped out until one engaged me. Then, hooked, I moved to the mezzanine and disappeared from view. I've no memory of what I read during that period, as if my mind has squirrelled away the characters, plots and places, hidden them behind closed doors to which I have no key.

I do remember when *he* first appeared. I thought he was like me, another reader seeking solitude. His dark, curly hair framed a face of serious intent as he turned the pages of his book.

He didn't speak and I got used to him being there whenever I was. On occasions, when I glanced up, he caught my eye, smiled and nodded. I wondered who he was.

When I was fifteen and poised on the threshold of womanhood and sexual awareness, I fell upon *Pride and Prejudice*. I was moved by Austen's story of human weakness, betrayal and love, and the unforgettable moment of understanding and union between Elizabeth and Darcy. As I turned its last page, *he* spoke to me for the first time. 'Have you thought about writing a book?' As usual, he was sitting opposite. I was startled for I had got used to his silent, Adonis presence.

'No,' I replied.

'I think you may have a gift.'

'How can you tell?'

'The way you read. As if your life depended on it. The power of words moves you.'

I blushed. The thought of having been observed with such scrutiny was unsettling.

'You should try writing.' With that, he got up and left.

I was taken aback by the abruptness but wondered if I *could* write. Later the same day, I stopped at the Post Office and picked out a hardbacked notebook with a flowery cover.

At home, I opened it and wrote *Thelma Lea's Writings* on the inside.

It took some time to get started. What to write? How to write? I had only done work for school before – essays, poems in the style of, exam questions. This wasn't the same.

After several failed attempts and pages covered in crossed-out words, I put the notebook to one side, deciding to take it with me the next time I went to the library.

'How did you get on?' he asked, as I took my seat a few days later.

'Not very well.'

'Do you want some help?'

'Yes, please.'

'Close your eyes.' His voice was soft.

I hesitated before shutting them, embarrassed but filled with a sense of anticipation.

'What do you see?'

'Nothing.'

'Relax. Breathe slowly. Let your imagination flow. I'll take you on a journey.'

I slowed my breathing, became aware of the muffled sounds of the library and the traffic passing outside, of my hands resting on the table.

'Imagine being under a waterfall. It's crashing down around you. The spray dampens your face. Sunlight dances. It's a warm day. You are looking for something. Go and explore.'

As his voice faded, I found myself behind a cascade of water. Far below me, it splashed and surfed. Spray caught the sun. I turned to my right, inched along the slippery path to the outer edge of the fall. Snow-topped mountains surrounded me. A spring bubbled from a rock face. I cupped my hands in it and drank.

'Now write.' His voice brought me back to the library.

I opened my eyes, took my pen and began. I wrote of a young woman, an intrepid lone adventurer on a quest, discovering the wonders and perils of a mountainous landscape, searching for a long-lost uncle, the only person who could tell her what happened to her family and the land that once belonged to them …

When I next looked up, the library was closing and his seat was empty.

After that day, my waking moments and solitary walks were filled with ideas, conversations and characters from my book – fragments to be integrated in the writing.

When I went to the library, I told him everything. He listened and smiled and asked questions.

One morning, when I awoke, he was sitting in the wicker chair next to my bed, one leg crossed over the other, watching me.

I gasped. But before I could speak, there was a knock and Mother came in with a mug of tea. 'It's seven o'clock. Come on, time to get up. You'll be late.'

I held my breath, waiting for her to notice him.

She walked right past, set the mug on my desk, turned and went out, calling behind her, 'Don't forget to bring the laundry down when you come.'

When she'd gone, he said, 'It's just you and me.'

'Wh … who *are* you?' I asked.

He hesitated before replying, uncrossed his legs, sat up straight. 'You.'

I stared.

'It happens. Don't be afraid.'

Today, I have friends and family but I suffer what can only be described as a fragmentation of self. While I appear whole on the outside, each fragment inside pulls in a different direction, like a mirror shattering over and over, reflecting me in splinters. *He* is a splinter grown large.

We sit in the library. I take comfort from his presence.

We walk across the Downs and into the woods beyond, stand on the ledge at the end of the line of trees overlooking the Avon Gorge, watch the brown ribbon of water flow below. I have no urge to lean forward and embrace the force of gravity, only the desire to write.

Look up before you enter Bristol's Central Library, and meet the gaze of Chaucer, Father of English Poetry. He is the central figure in the first of three relief sculptures in the lunette niches above the oriel windows. Beside him are some of his Canterbury pilgrims: the Prioress, the Wife of Bath – silenced in stone – the Knight, the Miller, the Merchant and the Man of Law. In the central lunette is the first English historian, the Venerable Bede. He is flanked by literary saints: St Aidan, St Chad, St Augustine, St Cuthbert, St Paulinus and Caedmon. In the final lunette is King Alfred, the Father of English Prose and promoter of universal education. With him are early chroniclers: an unnamed minstrel, Cynewulf the wandering bard, St Gildas, William of Malmesbury, Florence of Worcester and Wace the Norman minstrel. All three groups are by the Bristol-born sculptor Charles Pibworth, who received £475 for the work.

The Rose, the Shamrock and the Thistle – images representing different parts of the United Kingdom – decorate the library's gables, while, at the bottom of each oriel, panels of vines, grapes and figs symbolise the Tree of Knowledge. These are the work of the sculptor William Aumonier, who carved in situ the escutcheon above the main doorway displaying the arms of the City of Bristol. The door arch is decorated with a garland of bay laurel and berries, an emblem of Apollo, god of the Arts, Eloquence and Useful Sciences.

Paper, pen and ink.
Very simple instruments
to capture our lives.

The Book Room

Gail Swann

'I must say, this is a right pick 'n' mix for a rough boy like you.'

Gloria, they called him. Book Room Monitor, it said on his badge, attached with a plastic crocodile clip to his Trusty-green polo shirt. 'I'm frankly impressed if you've actually read all these in a week.'

Conversation at the check-in counter was something new. Dan braced himself. Monitors came and went, but he had not encountered this one before. Except by reputation.

'Why wouldn't I read them, and what's it to you?'

'Jump down my throat, why don't you?' The Trusty appeared to blink away his disdain, flaunting a smudge of kohl amongst the creases around his eyes. 'A book-savvy con is like smoked salmon amongst the fish fingers. I had high hopes for you.' He rummaged in a tray of dog-eared cards. 'You know at my last place we did this with barcodes. I can't believe how crude the system is here.' He was older, close up, than he looked when he was parading around the wing with his gay entourage.

'Do you make it a habit to insult the punters?' Dan said. 'You're on your own here.'

'The buffer of a nice high counter gives one a certain confidence.' But Dan could see it wasn't that. They were about the same medium height, but where Dan was lean in youth, Gloria was sinewy, overworked muscles compacted into a powerful body. He moved with swinging shoulders and his chest thrust out. Defying age and assailants.

Dan shrugged and half turned away while he waited, his eyes

drifting along the rows of low-level bookcases to a bank of tables occupied by a handful of cons wearing red shirts, like Dan's. The rank and file. Only one appeared to be reading, others staring into space or whispering to each other. Not a club he cared to join. *Nowhere to lose yourself except inside your head.* Dan sighed and turned back to face the Book Room Monitor.

'It wouldn't be much of a barrier if you really upset someone,' he said idly.

'Oh, don't forget our friends up there.' Gloria waved at a CCTV camera, one of several, providing full coverage of the room.

'A lot can happen in a few seconds.'

'Don't worry yourself over me, pet. The nasty boys don't come in here. Books are for poofs or something like that.' He held out Dan's ticket allocation then retracted the little green cards when Dan went to take them. 'Present company excepted, mind.' Gloria's hand hovered, brushing against the hair on Dan's wrist. 'Shame though. Rough boy with a brain, mmm, so rare in this dive.'

Dan shuddered. He had no inclination to learn why even the most notorious cons showed respect to this camp old lifer with his affectations and dyed-blond buzz cut.

'Quit with your flirting. I'm only interested in the books. I'm not game for you or anyone else, right?'

'Feisty boy. How rousing.' The Trusty clamped his free hand around Dan's wrist, pinning it to the counter top. Dan inhaled sharply but didn't flinch or pull away.

'Not scared of you,' he whispered. 'Get the fuck off me.'

'Just taking a look at this splendid tattoo,' Gloria called out, for the benefit of the CCTV cameras.

'Shuddup, would ya,' an obese red-shirt grunted from a nearby aisle. A couple of others who'd just entered the room chuckled as they walked past the counter.

'Button your bulbous lips, lard boy,' Gloria snarled, then softly back to Dan: 'Just a peek, what's the harm?'

Dan glared at him but didn't move his arm when the Trusty relinquished his grip. 'I hope it brightens your day, but could you hurry up, I'm on the clock here.'

'Tattoos used to be my Achilles' heel you know.' He studied Dan's arm. 'There's a story in this, isn't there? Rock idols and women and botany, for starters.'

'It's a thistle. Scottish roots.'

'Oh, a hot Scot … you're a right little page turner. Could you elaborate on the meaning of the rest of this masterpiece?'

'A mate of mine was a trainee tattooist. He used my arm to practise on and tried to cram a lot in. It means fuck all.'

'You're a lousy fibber, pet. No one has a random face etched into their skin. So who's the *femme fatale*?'

'I'd rather not be reminded. Can I have the tickets?'

But Gloria held on to them as he leaned forward, speaking in a low voice without the elaborations of his persona. 'If you're going to be here a long time, and I can see from that haunted aura that you are, you must work on your back story.'

'What are you talking about?'

'Your starkness pains me, boy. The struggle to stay afloat in the wash of prison life, whiplashed daily by your own worthlessness. Am I right?'

'If you say so.' Dan was suddenly conscious of the lack of space between them. He stepped away from the counter, changing the angle from which he was being observed by the unseen wardens.

'Shutting out reality with a good novel is a great help, of course.' Gloria picked up a book from a nearby trolley and opened it on the counter, turning it towards Dan, as if they were debating its content. He glanced up at the CCTV, smiling, and kept his voice low. 'But it's not enough. You need to create a fiction of your own. Mystery is always alluring. Drip feed an enticing personal history into the minutiae of wing-life and deference will find you. Far less vexing than using violence.'

'I suppose this bullshit worked for you, did it?'

'From the scattering of a few seeds a long time ago.' He cocked a pruned eyebrow. 'They're not big on reading, but the lamebrains cling to rumour and gossip like limpets. Cram it in, rough boy, like your tattooist friend. You said yourself, it means fuck all.'

'Acting's not my thing. I'm not a sociopath.'

'Ouch, what a pernicious little barb.' Gloria turned his head to the side, tossing away the insult. Behind his left ear, lurking beneath thinning hair, Dan glimpsed an old tattoo of a leggy black spider. 'My alter ego has served me well in the past three establishments.' Empathy had vanished from his tone. 'Before that, well, wouldn't you like to know?'

'So where would I find the autobiography? Fact or fiction section?'

'You're a vexatious smartarse.' The Book Room Monitor slammed shut the hardback on the desk. A murmured exclamation rippled around the room. Dan stood still as Gloria fanned out the tickets on the counter, fingering them, not quite relinquishing them.

'It's a hollow life,' he finally said, his pale eyes fixed on Dan's, 'if you insist on going it alone.'

'I'm all right, thanks.' Dan gently collected the tickets, half expecting to have them snatched away again. There were people behind them now; someone's fetid breath, shuffling feet and grunts of impatience.

'Next!' Gloria chimed.

It took a few minutes for Dan's heartbeat to slow as he made for the farthest bookshelves. Every day in prison he kept company with hard men and weirdos, vulnerable halfwits and frightened once-ordinary citizens. He mused about the lives of this cast of characters when the lights were out and boredom crushed him. But he did not want Gloria in that epic novel.

'If the dame takes a likin' to you … watch your back, kid,' a grizzled old red-shirt whispered hoarsely as Dan passed by the table bank.

'Yeah, I get that.' But the man had returned to ogling a porn magazine secreted inside a copy of *National Geographic*. Dan's eyes went to the CCTV but the reader had seated himself strategically. Another con bumped hard against his shoulder. 'Sucker,' he hissed. Wiping spittle from his face, Dan understood that *library* was missing from the name of this place for good reason. Peace, reflection and self-improvement were more likely to be found in the toilet block.

He skim-read a few back covers. The Book Room Monitor's scrutiny burned him from across the room whenever the counter was quiet. Devoid of focus, Dan decided quickly on three titles and took them to be checked out. *Get it over with.*

'You have a delicious bitterness in your dark chocolate eyes,' Gloria said cheerfully, back to his posturing self, 'and street life in your complexion. I do so love a bit of coarse.'

'I'm flattered.'

'Did you kill him with your bare hands?'

'I didn't kill anyone.'

'Shame. I think you'd get away with saying you did. That cloak of brooding menace that draws itself about you … oh my.'

'Quit, would you? The books …'

'The woman on your arm. It was all about her, wasn't it? A crime of passion.'

'No …'

'Jealousy. Murderous rage. I know you've got it in you.'

'Fuck off.' But Dan was stifling a grin, worn down by the relentless drama.

'There is nothing to be ashamed of in the platitudes of humanity.' Gloria smiled widely in an exposé of bright white dentures. 'The same old stories, ancient as mankind, perpetually re-told and dark. Always dark.'

'Pitch black,' Dan agreed, and placed his selection on the counter.

'What delights do we have here?' Gloria shook open the books and placed them one on top of the other. 'All the thrills of a lucky dip. *The Diary of a Nobody*; that won't do much for your self-esteem, boy. *Overthrown by Strangers*; well that can happen all too easily in here, I can't think why you'd want to read about it.' Dan's grin broke finally at Gloria's commentary. '*A Stained White Radiance*. Well …' He stamped each title with a flourish. 'No one's going to stove your head in to get their hands on these, that's for sure.'

'Yeah, for once in my life it pays to have nothing of value.'

'Nothing but the boy, hmm.' Gloria closed the books. The playfulness seemed to leach out of his lined face as he smoothed their saggy plastic covers.

'I've gotta get to work. Lunch prep.' Dan leaned over the counter and saw that Gloria's hands were clasped over the pile.

'You do have something of value, pet.' The old con's eyes had taken on a milky sheen. 'And I suggest you lend it out, like you would a good book to a deserving friend … then no one has to steal it.' Elsewhere in the room someone sniggered. *Overthrown by Strangers*.

'It's a book room not a bloody brothel!' The proclamation was barked from a crackly speaker on Gloria's workbench behind the counter, making both men jump. 'If I have to come down there …'

'Don't disturb yourself, sir,' Gloria said to the CCTV. 'My fire is doused. Your omnipotence is as effective as any sprinkler system.'

'Just do your job, Trusty, or you'll be having hot flushes in the laundry instead.'

'No peace for the wicked,' Gloria huffed, and thrust the books towards Dan. 'I haven't had a fish in a pot for a while,' he growled. 'I'm just trying to save this boy from the auspices of lesser mortals.' The speaker returned no comment and the Book Room was as silent as a proper library.

Dan gathered his books, holding them tight against his red shirt like a protective breastplate. He would need all his wits to avoid getting tangled up in Gloria's long-running soap opera.

'I'm no stranger to your kind,' he said. 'You remind me of someone in particular. His downfall was big news if you moved in those kind of circles. He didn't see it coming. Never underestimate the quiet ones. I don't need your babysitting.'

'Get out of there, McGinley, before I put you on report.' The speaker delivered another disembodied reprimand.

Gloria rubbed his hands together, magnanimous once more. 'I'm touched that you're taking my advice. I can get you a new tattoo started. That other arm is so bare.'

He fingered the age-blurred black and red spider by his ear. 'Round one to you then, *Mr McGinley*. Having unearthed you, my little book worm, I'm not about to queer my pitch, as it were.'

'End of chapter, then.' Dan walked away.

The distance from the counter to the exit felt like a vast expanse. Dan sensed that all the cons in the Book Room were walking him out with furtive amusement, and maybe, if he was lucky, a little grudging respect. As he pushed open the door, Gloria called out breezily: 'Same time next week, rough boy.'

As Dan hurried away to mundane tasks, he resolved to research the habits of the black widow spider before his books were due back to the place they didn't call a library.

Step inside the Central Library to the green marble entrance hall, like a church crypt with its low wide arches. The atmosphere is serious; you are here to study and to learn. Ahead – enlightenment, symbolised by the pool of light over the Grand Staircase.

I browse. Behind me
a whole universe awaits
my discovery.

The Judge's Chair

Jean Burnett

The mind plays tricks, especially in the dark, we all know that. And yet … and yet, I wish I could talk to JG again. Did we really hear anything at all? I know we didn't actually see anything … at least, I didn't. I'm not sure that I believe in the supernatural, life after death and all that stuff, but I don't disbelieve any more. My experience in the library changed all that.

I can still picture JG in his army fatigues sitting next to me in the computer room at the Central Library. He claimed to be descended from the poet Coleridge.

'Coleridge and Southey often used the Bristol library,' he told me, 'not the present Edwardian building; that came after their time.' JG, who was on extended leave from the army after a spell in Afghanistan, did not look the poetic type, but appearances can fool you. He had been suffering from post-traumatic stress disorder.

JG was a Bristolian born and bred while I was a London lad who had stayed on in the city after securing an indifferent degree from UWE. I hadn't been able to get a decent job so I waited tables at night and spent time in the computer room polishing my CV, surfing the net in search of a better life, and going down to the café for tuna rolls and weak coffee. At least there was company in the library. JG said he was addicted to computer dating, but he was just killing time.

'Do you ever go out with anyone, have you ever pulled?' I asked him once. All I got was one of his weird remarks. 'Why are there no gay people in Cheltenham?' This was followed by a suggestive laugh.

Outside the computer area the library oozed gothic atmosphere with its vaulted Reading Room and shadowy tiers of unread books. Surrounded by marble staircases and stained glass, amateur genealogists huddled over the Mormon archives. I enjoyed the atmosphere in a corny kind of way. JG knew a lot about the library.

'It's one of the oldest in the country,' he told me. 'It started as a chained library.'

He was an odd character – a squaddie who liked poetry. 'That's not so unusual,' he said when I asked him about it. 'Soldiers often read in quiet times. Our sergeant liked Jane Austen. I'm not kidding.'

I remember him, slumped over the computer, wearing a combination of khakis and a red sweater. His hair was beginning to thin – 'stress,' he said. In compensation, he was growing a narrow blond moustache. On warmer days he changed the sweater for a red shirt, its sleeves rolled up to show his military tattoos. Once he challenged me to show my own – just a small Celtic knot on the left bicep. He sniggered, 'Pansy!'

'So sit somewhere else,' I said. But he didn't.

It was through JG that I heard about the special room. I had glimpsed it through its glass doors – a sort of museum that was only opened on special occasions. When I peered through the glass, a bored librarian perked up at my apparent interest. She told me to join one of the guided tours later.

'You can get a good look at the old books and documents and other souvenirs collected over the centuries.' I could see ancient pieces of furniture, tall mahogany bookshelves, as well as the display cases full of leather-bound books. 'The overmantel was carved by Grinling Gibbons,' the librarian intoned.

Great.

'So, will you take a tour?' JG grinned. 'The room's supposed to be haunted.'

'Who haunts it?' I asked.

'Judge Jeffreys, "The Hanging Judge". You know – the one who convicted all the men from the Monmouth rebellion. It was a big deal around these parts in 1685. He was a vicious bastard. There's a tatty old chair that belonged to him near the fireplace. I wouldn't be surprised if my Coleridge ancestor flits about the shelves as well.'

'You're full of it,' I told him, and he was suddenly serious, leaning across my keyboard almost pushing his long, lean face into mine.

'You think I'm making this up, you pussy? Why don't we spend some time at night in the haunted room? Are you up for it, buddy? You never know, we might find the lost first edition of Kubla Khan. You know about that, don't you?'

'Yes, I do. I've got a degree in English literature, thank you very much.'

'No wonder you can't get work,' he grinned again and peered at my latest letter begging for a job. 'You get off on humiliation, don't you?'

'Yeah,' I replied, '"Been down so long it feels like up to me" – that's a quote.'

He cocked his head and looked at me seriously. 'We'd better find that first edition, or something else valuable. There's plenty of rare stuff in that room.'

Perhaps it was the gibe about my degree, or a kind of inferiority complex I had about JG being a hero of the Afghan conflict, but I was bored and I agreed. It was a stupid thing to do; we weren't teenagers. JG said he knew the library so well that it would be easy to hide somewhere until after closing time.

'How would we get into the room?' I asked.

JG said there wasn't a lock anywhere that he couldn't pick. 'My dad was a locksmith. I learned a lot from him.'

Was this another one of his stories? You had to take a lot on trust where JG was concerned.

Looking back, it was surprising there was no sophisticated alarm system to be set off by intruders. Perhaps Bristol City Council couldn't afford it. Anyway, nobody steals books any more – except JG.

On the agreed evening we crept out from an unused office on the top floor after a few hours of boredom, eating sandwiches from the café and listening to JG describing life on the front line.

'Only one set of body armour between three, a gimpy that keeps jamming, a hundred pounds on your back, forty-two degrees in the shade – if there was any – and all for three pounds fifty an hour.'

'Why do you do it?'

I shone the torchlight on his face and he gave one of his manic grins. 'For Queen and country o' course! Let's go.'

It was ten pm as we made our way towards the reference library with the aid of a torch and the occasional security light. The cosy, Edwardian atmosphere had given way to one of uneasy gothic gloom as darkness closed around us, perfumed with the scent of paper and leather and photocopying chemicals.

There was a penetrating chill in the air which contrasted with the overheated daytime atmosphere. A girl friend once dragged me to see one of those Twilight films and I half expected a few grey-faced, vampiric librarians to appear from behind the enquiry desk.

JG picked the lock on the glass doors with ease. In the room, at first, I was aware only of heaviness – the weight of the stuffy, velvety darkness in a place that didn't get any fresh air. You could almost touch it. I took out my mobile to boost the faltering light of my torch. It was dead. I shook it, stabbing at the buttons. It was useless. I could hear JG breathing loudly.

'Try your mobile,' I whispered urgently. I shone the torch at him and he shook his head. It was probably just an odd co-incidence, I told myself.

After a few moments of groping around a display case JG grabbed my arm and whispered, 'Did you hear that?'

I shook him off. 'Stop playing the fool. Of course I didn't hear anything.'

He grabbed the torch and whispered in my ear; 'The breathing, man, can't you hear it?'

'Stop it, you prick,' I whispered back. 'It's you.'

'No!' he hissed. 'It came from over there.' Why were we whispering? It's just something you do in the dark in a strange place. I knocked my shin against something hard.

'Shine the torch ahead, mate,' I whispered, but he seemed reluctant to do that, as if he didn't want to see what the light would show him. He was beginning to annoy me. No, he was beginning to spook me. Why had I agreed to such a bloody pointless expedition? There was nothing to gain from breaking into a library.

'Think of that first edition,' JG had said, but we had as much chance of finding a lost masterpiece in that black vault as I had of finding a worthwhile job. Anyway, I was not a thief and JG was all talk. He said his poet ancestor had been a rebel and would approve of our dare. I recalled that Coleridge had been some kind of drug addict – opium, wasn't it? Narcotics in other words; that was probably the only thing JG had in common with him. It would account for his crazy behaviour. I wrenched the torch from his hand as he stopped dead again.

'Listen! Can't you hear it – the breathing?' JG's voice rose; he was beginning to sound afraid, this man who had fought in various hellish parts of the world, 'All around the sandbox, man, the Gulf, Iraq, Afghanistan …'

That was when the atmosphere really started to affect me. Of course, it was all the fault of JG's play acting. He was trying to wind me up. Whatever I felt or heard or didn't hear, I decided I had had enough. I grasped his hand and tried to pull him towards where I thought the doors must be, but I couldn't move him. He was stiff and frozen and I could feel the fear coming off him although I couldn't see his face.

Somehow, I managed to drag him a few yards with one hand while shining the feeble torchlight in the other. This was done without a word spoken. He seemed to be struck dumb and I couldn't, for some reason, break the ticking silence in the room. It was then I realised we were not heading for the door. I raised the torch and saw this massive black, carved mantelpiece looming out of the wall and the tattered armchair just a few feet in front of us.

I sensed a presence and I heard rasping breathing like a rusty door hinge, and what could have been a low chuckle. Then, from the direction of the old armchair a voice said loudly and distinctly, 'Damn you!'

I jumped back, feeling as if the blood had stopped moving in my veins and some invisible hand was squeezing my heart. The pain was terrible for a few seconds that seemed like an hour.

I've tried to blot out the memories of those moments, but they come back to me in the middle of the night, or on dark roads when I'm walking home alone. I can't be sure that I saw anything, but I must have clutched at JG because he suddenly came to life, uttering a high-pitched scream like an animal. He threw off my hand and fled away from the chair. I followed him blindly, panic rising. I cracked my shins against all kinds of obstacles but, somehow, we were through the glass doors. Before I dropped the torch and everything went black I saw JG curled up in a ball by the open door, twitching and muttering.

As I groped for the torch I tripped and banged my head against the enquiry desk, and almost knocked myself out. Groggily, I felt for JG, grabbing his leg. He screamed again. I desperately wanted to be away from that spot. I felt for my mobile in my pocket – and it worked fine.

JG was in no state to be led out of the building. I doubted I could get him to move at all, let alone pick another lock, and somehow the thought of feeling my way down that winding, white staircase in the dark made my skin crawl. Fear drove out everything except the urge to get help. I fumbled at the digits with trembling fingers, hitting wrong numbers.

'What service do you require?' a voice said when I got through. What could I say … 'I bashed my head, and my friend is gibbering?' I muttered something about being in shock and explained where we were. The light from my mobile was the only thing I could see; no moon or starlight shone through the windows. Then I remembered there were no windows in that part of the building.

In the ghastly minutes before our rescuers arrived a quotation from Nathanial Hawthorne kept running through my head, 'In the depths of every heart there is a tomb and a dungeon.' Who knows what we keep in that place? JG had stopped muttering; then he chuckled – at least, I think it was JG. The glass door was still open.

By the time the emergency services arrived, together with the library caretaker, neither of us was very coherent. We were taken to hospital but I was released after a few hours while JG was kept in for observation. The police warned me that I could be charged with breaking and entering, but the library did not press charges. Later I received a stern letter from the chief librarian saying I was banned for life from entering the place.

Soon after, I left Bristol for good and returned to London. My local library is in a shopping mall and refreshingly free of atmosphere.

I wish I could speak to JG and compare notes, but it's too late now. After he recovered he was sent back to Afghanistan. Three months later I heard on TV that he had been blown up by a roadside bomb in Helmand province. I watched his coffin coming home through Wootton Bassett.

I never discovered if he was really related to Coleridge.

On the right of the Central Library entrance hall are two doors. In 1906 the first led to the newspaper room where job seekers scanned the situations vacant columns and the city's prostitutes consulted Lloyds lists to see what ships (and prospective clients) were due into the docks.

I touch the book, and
the dust of ages rises
around my fingers.

Lost In France

Ali Bacon

When Alec woke his watch said six thirty. He'd left home on Monday and taken the night ferry. He knew he was in France, but which day was it now? He got up and went to the door of the old coachhouse and looked up the drive to where the chateau made a pale outline against an amethyst sky. From the syrupy warmth of the air he decided it was dusk. He had only slept for a couple of hours.

On the ancient chest of drawers lay a bunch of keys handed to him that morning by Lucien, the owner of the chateau. Alec, still groggy from the journey, had barely listened to what he had said. He had no concept of what he had taken on: the house, the estate, how big the responsibility might be. It all felt as crazy as it had back in Oxford when his supervisor first mentioned it. A small chateau with a stash of rare books, a chance to get some original research under his belt in exchange for a couple of months' work in the chateau garden.

It was the same day he'd bumped into Isobel Grant. He hadn't seen her since they were undergrads, but apparently she worked at the Bodleian now. He'd told her the job sounded like heaven. On his way home, reality kicked in.

How could he possibly take off to France all summer, on his own? He'd hardly dared even mention the idea to Julia. But when he did, she was all for it.

'You should go. It might give the bloody thesis a shot in the arm.' She was folding nappies, flushed with the exertion of lugging washing up to the flat from the garden, still carrying a bit of baby weight. 'I'll stay at Mum's for a while. She and Dad are desperate to see more of Robbie. We'll save money. And you need a break.' She ran her hand through her hair. 'We both do.'

But saying goodbye to her and Robbie on the station platform had been an act of violence, a ripping apart of the fragile membrane that bound them as a family, like stripping Elastoplast from tender skin. As the shadows deepened to purple, Alec thought of them both, their combined smell, their mother and child indivisibility.

Self-pity wasn't going to help. From the gates at the end of the drive, he saw a wide street with tidy bungalows on either side, a bus stop and at the far end a squat church. It could be any of the trillions of unremarkable villages that spattered the empty areas of France. But there were signs of life. Opposite the bus stop he spotted a striped canopy and above it the neon sign *Brasserie*. His spirits lifted. A bottle of wine would dull the harsh voice in his ear that said this had been a terrible mistake.

Stepping inside the café, Alec experienced the tangible resistance to any newcomer in a French drinking place. Not fancying his chances at the *comptoir,* he nodded to its silent occupants and pointed to where an internal door had been removed and a hand-written sign attached to the lintel saying *Restaurant.*

'*On peut manger?*'

One of the men went behind the bar and put his head round another door. '*Un peu de service ici!*'

In the back room there was a smell of onions and scorched butter. The menu card was dog-eared and bore two blobs of oil. Alec sat down at one of the tables. The wallpaper, dotted with posies of blue flowers, was at odds with the geometric carpet and bentwood chairs. The room felt oddly domestic.

A girl came to take his order. She had a round pale face with wide-set eyes, a deep fringe and long hair in a ponytail. She laid a basket of bread in front of him that he guessed would be stale. When she spoke her voice had a sing-song cadence put on for customers.

He ordered *poulet frites* and confined himself to a small carafe of red. Getting blotto wouldn't be clever. The girl walked away, and he watched her ponytail swing in time with her hips.

When she came back with the food she smiled at him and asked if he was working at *le château*. Alec nodded. He felt her give him some kind of appraisal, but couldn't work out what her judgement might be. As he ate he could hear the conversation next door rising in volume and raucousness as the bar filled up.

As soon as he had finished eating he went back, wallet in hand, signifying his intention to pay. The girl was leaning on the counter, her arse jutting provocatively. Seeing Alec, she spoke to one of the men who was making bedroom eyes at her. He turned and offered his hand. This must be Henri Varenne, Lucien's estate manager and Alec's boss. Alec's hand disappeared into the workman's grip.

'*Alors*,' said the villager, '*à demain*.' As Alec left, the conversation behind him swelled with laughter. It didn't take much imagination to know the kind of comments being made. A fair-skinned academic, *un anglais*, wasn't expected to be much help around the local estate.

Back in his room the light was too dim for reading. He fell asleep but woke after only an hour. He tried to conjure Julia, at ease in his arms, her hand straying towards his stiffening cock. But suddenly the imaginary mouth beneath his belonged to the girl in the bar with the hips and the ponytail. Her tongue spoke back to him, French kissing for real. He turned his pillow over, searching for coolness, and came face to face with Isobel Grant. In that café in Oxford, long fingers spread out on the table. The persistent curiosity of her yellow-green eyes had made him curious back. He told her about the chateau and she said she was going to Brittany for a couple of weeks with her family. When the details of the job came through, Alec had photocopied the map, scrawled 'In case you're passing!'

on the bottom and dropped it off at the Bodleian. He couldn't think why he'd done it. But it hardly mattered; Isobel would not come. Even if she'd got his note, Brittany was a hundred miles away, in the wrong direction.

Her image appeared before him now. A skimpy T-shirt poked into points by small breasts. He adjusted the picture so that she was coming towards him from the beach, her skin salty and roughened with sand, the three triangles of a bikini tied at the edges, easily undone to reveal the pale untouchable places underneath. He rode out the fantasy, catching its sticky outcome in his hand. When he'd cleaned himself up he thumped the pillow into submission and fell asleep.

If Henri and Alec had nothing in common it didn't seem to matter. Out in the gardens Alec did what he was told; he even enjoyed the unaccustomed exercise. And as soon as Henri downed tools, usually around two, Alec headed for the library.

It was a gem of a place and he had it to himself. Original editions from the seventeenth century crowded the walls, right up to a gallery reached by a tiny spiral staircase. The writers, mainly women, had almost invented the love story. But the writing was coy, cryptic, infuriating. Alec spent hours teasing out parlour-game poetry, untangling names and soubriquets, working out the alliances, the political and romantic manoeuvrings, the betrayals. When his brain had had enough he would pile up his books on the corner of the dainty escritoire and write a letter to Julia. He kept her replies in the library too, since no one else went there, and soon he had a little stack of them. The graze inflicted by their parting was less raw now, like the soft patch of skin on Robbie's head that had eventually firmed over. At night the women in his bed, Julia, Isobel, any of the girls he might spot in the café or the local market, were interchangeable. As a lover he was languorous or hectic, adoring or sometimes cruel. None of it mattered. He was alone with his fantasies. The world outside had disappeared.

After three weeks a letter came from Julia that was different from the others. She had had enough of being with her parents. It was claustrophobic and Robbie was being spoiled silly. She was rested and ready to get back to Oxford.

Alec was glad she was going back. He was reminded again of the strength she seemed to draw from the child, now that he was past the tiny baby stage. With the letter she enclosed a lock of Robbie's hair, to show him how much it had grown. The baby hair was soft between his fingers, blonder than Alec remembered. Lightened by the sun, perhaps; even in England, it was summertime.

Perhaps he should go home too. They had had their break, their time apart. The library here was engrossing, but most of the books could probably be sourced in Oxford. At the end of the week he would have been here a month. Lucien had already buggered off to the *Midi*, but surely he could contact him and ask to be released?

Once the thought had crossed his mind it was hard to shake off. Too distracted to study, he locked up the library and went over to the coachhouse where, if he remembered rightly, he still had a train timetable stuffed in the bottom of his holdall. Yes, there was a twice-daily service from Saumur to the ferry at Caen. He could ring the ferry company from the main house right now and be home in a matter of days. The thought of seeing Robbie and being with Julia, the real Julia, hit him like a punch in the gut and he sat down on the edge of the bed. First things first. He didn't want to muddy the waters with his tutor. Lucien had to agree, and for that he needed Henri on his side. Their relationship had got better since their first awkward encounter. He would speak to him tonight in the café.

With his mind made up there wasn't much point going back to the library. He grabbed his sunglasses and a paperback he'd brought from home and went outside to the garden where he threw himself down next to the so-called *Grand Canal*, wondering at the hubris of the designer who had tried to ape Versailles in a remote corner of the Loire and ended up with no more than a stagnant lily pond.

Within a few minutes he was damp with sweat and could feel a headache coming on. There was a stone bench set against the wall of the house. He chose the end that was in the shade, but even here the heat was enervating. A pair of dragonflies was weaving a dance over the water. He closed the book and watched them, thinking of nothing.

He almost didn't see the girl coming up from the main gate. At least he thought it was a girl. The drive was overhung by laurels that created deep puddles of shadow and it was only as she stepped through the occasional patch of flickering sunlight that he could make her out. Yes, it was definitely a girl, but not one of the locals. She was wearing a peasant-style skirt and carried a hat in a way that conferred Englishness. For a crazy moment he thought that Julia had turned up to join him. Maybe she had felt as he had and jumped on a ferry that morning. So where on earth was Robbie?

But the stranger was too tall to be Julia, her hair too short and fluffy. Then, as she took the step that brought her from the overhanging shrubbery on to the path that flanked the pond, where the sun bounced crazily off the white gravel, Alec saw everything. How she was holding the brim of the hat in both hands, turning it methodically, a quarter of a turn at a time. And how between the fingers of one hand there was a folded sheet of paper gripped self-consciously, like a ticket. Like a map.

Fuck.

Isobel Grant was still hovering a little way off, as if she had reached some threshold she needed permission to cross. The hat was waving in his direction. 'Hi!'

Thank God for sunglasses. 'Hello!'

'Hope you don't mind. I really was passing, sort of.'

'Oh. Right. I mean, good. Great!'

'It wasn't as far as I expected. And I had the map.'

The bloody map. As she moved out of the sun and into focus she held it towards him, as if to say *this was your idea, remember?* He made room for her on the bench.

'Wow. What a place,' she said.

'How was Brittany?'

'Oh, you know. Ten days of rain, then the sun came out and we all got burned to a crisp.'

Under her strappy top her shoulders were pink. She fanned herself with the hat and looked across the pond to where the dragonflies still danced. Around her ankles there was a fine dusting of sand.

On the Grand Staircase, the Central Library's benefactor Vincent Stuckey Lean is commemorated with his coat of arms and his portrait. It was his bequest of £50,000 (more than £4 million in today's money) which enabled the city to build the library.

The Grand Staircase leads to the Exhibition Corridor, classical in design, and then to the Reference Library Reading Room, where daylight floods in through skylights in the high vaulted ceiling. Behind the ionic columns, spiral iron staircases lead to galleries on each side of the room.

Looking at the books
I feel the weight and passion
of our lives in words.

A Book By Its Cover

Jane Jones

Sweet sixteen, and never been kissed.

Nobody says that now, except as a joke. Girls grow up fast, much faster than in my day. And even then, there were girls who kissed, and more, when officially they were still considered children.

I wasn't one of them. Girls like me led decorous lives. On weekdays we walked or bicycled to our girls-only schools; on Saturdays we played hockey in winter or tennis in summer; on Sundays we attended Morning Prayer at church, and sometimes Evensong too. We wore woollen socks and sensible button-up shoes, and if we hankered after nylons and high heels we knew better than to say so to our parents. Mine, in particular, would not have sympathised with any such aspiration. I was their precious darling baby, the result of an unexpected late pregnancy when their three sons were already in their teens; they had no wish for me to grow up any faster than was absolutely necessary. At sixteen I still tied my hair in pigtails, and my beauty regime consisted of scrubbing my face with soap and water.

Naturally, then, I had never been kissed, except on the cheek by my mother, which doesn't count, and on the mouth once by Beryl Richards, at guide camp the previous summer, because we wanted to know how it felt. But that doesn't count either, because we were both girls.

I met Gerard on the third day of the Michaelmas term, on a sunny afternoon at the end of a fine, hot summer. He spotted me leaving school, and followed me into Woolworth's, and asked if he could buy me an ice-cream soda.

Looking back, it's easy to tut that I should have said no. I'd been warned about approaches from strange men often enough: what girl hasn't? But somehow Gerard didn't seem strange to me; somehow, it was as if I already knew him. It wasn't just because he was handsome. When he smiled at me, I felt a connection. I smiled back. My face made the decision on its own, before I had even thought about it.

Over the ice-cream soda, he asked if I'd ever thought of becoming an actress. I laughed. I thought he was flattering me, trying to get me to like him. Couldn't he see that I liked him already?

'I'm serious, Pam,' he said. 'I work at Lemville Studios; I'm production assistant on a film that could be really big, if we get the casting right. But the storyline involves a schoolgirl who swaps places with a showgirl, and we can't find an actress who looks convincing in both roles. Put them in fishnets and lipstick, and they're fine; put them in gymslips and wash off the make-up ...' He sighed. 'We've auditioned twenty-four so far, and not one of them could carry it off. The director's even been talking about abandoning the project altogether. Then last week I had an idea: what if, instead of searching for an actress who can play a schoolgirl, we just cast a real schoolgirl?'

I felt my smile falter. I could be useful to him – that was the reason he had approached me. Not because he liked me. Not because he was interested in me in any more personal way. Of course not! How stupid of me, to imagine that a man like Gerard ...

He reached across the table and squeezed my hand. 'The rest of the team thought I was crazy. They said I'd never find anyone suitable. I had to admit it was a long shot, but nobody else had any better ideas, so I started looking. And today I saw you.'

I didn't trust myself to speak. I stared down at my empty sundae glass.

From the corner of my eye I could see his hand resting on mine.

He had taken off his jacket, and the cuff of his shirt sleeve was turned up. His suntanned forearm was veiled with dark hair.

'I saw you,' he repeated. 'And I thought, if that girl can be taught to act … she's the one. I know about these things; I've been working in Hollywood for the last three years.'

Beneath the table, his foot brushed against my shoe. Maybe it was an accident, but maybe it wasn't; maybe he really did like me, as well as wanting me to be in his film.

I left my foot where it was, touching his. 'I've been in school plays and things. I was Major Barbara last year.'

'Shaw's *Major Barbara*? You had the leading role?' He was beaming now. 'That's marvellous! More than I'd dared hope! Of course, you'd still need training – quite intensive training, because acting for the camera's very different from acting on stage. But that's something the studio can easily arrange.'

'I don't know if my parents would let me. They want me to do my Higher School Certificate, and then train as a nurse.' It was what I'd wanted myself, until then; I'd never wanted to be an actress of any kind, film or stage. I wasn't at all sure I wanted to be one now.

He nodded sympathetically. 'Parents can be tricky, at your age. We'll have to be careful to handle them the right way.'

The secret, he said, was to take it slowly. The worst thing I could do would be to rush home and tell them at once; they would only dismiss it as nonsense, and convince themselves I had been taken in by some smooth-talking scoundrel. The very idea would provoke such prejudice and mistrust that they might never come round to it. Instead, I should bide my time and say absolutely nothing to anyone until I had the firm offer of a film contract. Then my parents would have no option but to give the idea the serious consideration it deserved.

'And once they see what a wonderful opportunity it could be for you, Pam, I'm sure they won't raise any objections. Especially when they realise how much money you stand to make.' A wry half-smile dimpled the corners of his mouth. 'If the screen test goes the way I expect, you could be a very wealthy young lady by the time you turn twenty-one.'

'Really?'

'Oh, yes. Very wealthy indeed, provided your father gets a lawyer to check the contract before you sign anything. But please don't tell anyone at the studio I said that!'

I was young; I thought riches could only bring happiness. I thought if I never saw Gerard again, I might die of misery. By the time we parted that afternoon, I had agreed to a screen test.

It was to take place the following weekend. I had to go to a Guide rally first, so Gerard said he would arrange for a cameraman to come out to Danemouth to save me travelling all the way to the studio. He said my Girl Guide uniform wouldn't matter, and might even be an advantage as it would create more of a contrast with the showgirl shots. And I wasn't to worry about those as the studio would send a professional make-up artist to help me, and provide a suitable costume. He said he was sure I would look the part perfectly.

On the day of the screen test he was waiting for me at the back door of the Majestic Hotel as planned. The cameraman had been delayed, so Gerard had decided to film the showgirl section first. That way, the make-up artist could use the waiting time to get me ready.

When he took me upstairs to meet her, she looked me up and down, and shook her head.

'This girl won't do. She bites her fingernails.'

Gerard frowned. 'Does that matter? Surely such a tiny detail isn't – '

'The details count!' she snapped. 'They have to be right! You can't just ignore them.'

I thought she was very rude to speak to her boss so abruptly, and it wasn't if my nails were chewed halfway down to the cuticle like Lilian Ridgeway's. They were only a little bit nibbled. 'I don't bite them very much,' I said, 'and I can easily stop if I want to. It shouldn't take more than about a fortnight for them to grow back.'

'But we can't wait a fortnight!' Gerard sounded desperate. I guessed his director was still threatening to cancel the film. 'You know we can't, Josie! Everything's set up for tonight; if we put it off, there might never be another chance. Surely there must be something you can do?'

Josie relented. She took my hands and inspected them carefully. 'All right. I'll try. The result won't be perfect, but it should be good enough to pass as long as no one checks too closely.'

After that she became very friendly, and took a lot of trouble to make me look the way she said the director wanted. I didn't want to risk upsetting her again so I let her do whatever she liked, even put peroxide on my hair. She said a blonde wig wouldn't look natural enough for the close-ups, and she'd give me a brunette rinse afterwards to turn my hair dark again.

'Well?' she said when she'd finished, turning me to face a cheval glass in the corner of the room. 'What do you think of yourself?'

I didn't know what to think.

Except that the girl in the mirror was not me.

The girl in the mirror had platinum blonde hair that tumbled over her bare shoulders in fat sausage curls. She had scarlet lips and scarlet nails, bright against pale powdered skin and a shimmering white evening gown. Her wide, black-rimmed eyes stared out at me from beneath plucked and pencilled brows.

I took a step towards the glass, and stumbled; the girl in the mirror did the same. I looked down, and saw my own scarlet toenails peeping out of high-heeled silver sandals.

Josie tweaked the skirt of my gown where a spangle had come loose. 'The make-up's far too heavy for everyday wear, of course. But you're supposed to look like a showgirl, remember?'

'And ... do I?'

'Oh, yes.' She was smirking. 'Shall we call Gerard in, and show him the transformation?'

Just for a moment, when Gerard first saw me, he looked stunned. Literally stunned, as if someone had punched him. His mouth went slack, and his eyes flicked from me to Josie and back again. And just for that moment, I was frightened.

But then he clapped his hands and told me I was 'spectacular', 'amazing', 'incredible', a 'star in the making'. When Josie went to see if the cameraman had arrived, he locked the door and opened a bottle of champagne. I thought the way he'd looked at me might be just the way men look when they see a woman they want to kiss, and the thought made me melt inside, because I wanted him to kiss me. I wanted it more than I'd ever wanted anything in my life.

He poured champagne into two glasses, and offered one to me. I took it. He raised his glass, and said, 'Here's to you, Pam! To a brilliant future as a star of the silver screen!'

I raised my own glass and said, 'And to you, too. For making it happen.'

He smiled. 'To us!'

We drank the champagne. It was sharp and sweet at the same time, and so cold it almost hurt my mouth. The bubbles made me tingle all over. And I was waiting and waiting for him to kiss me, but he didn't.

So I kissed him.

I could tell it took him by surprise, but he didn't pull away. He let me kiss him, and he kissed me back, although he didn't put his tongue in my mouth the way Beryl did when we experimented that time. We kissed for ages, and when we finally broke off he said, 'I'm afraid the champagne might have gone to your head, young lady.'

He was looking at me very intently, his dark eyes questioning. To reassure him that I knew what I was doing, that he wasn't taking advantage of me, I put my arms round his neck and pulled him close. 'It's all right! There's no need to worry; I'm not drunk.'

When I said it, I thought it was true. I thought the feeling of giddiness was just the excitement of kissing him. But suddenly the floor seemed to tilt beneath my feet, and if Gerard hadn't been holding me so tightly I would have fallen over. The champagne seemed to rise in my throat, and I didn't like the taste any more.

There was a couch against the wall behind me. Gerard pushed me towards it.

'No,' I said. The whole room was spinning now and I was afraid if I lay down it would only get worse. 'I don't want – '

'Don't fight this, Pam.' His breath was hot on my neck. 'Just relax. Let yourself go.'

My legs gave way, and he lifted me on to the couch.

'Good girl,' he said. 'Lie there quietly, and it'll be easier for both of us. There's no turning back now. It shouldn't hurt much, as long as you co-operate.'

His hands went to my waist. I could feel him tugging and fumbling at the sash of my gown, untying it, pulling it loose …

I didn't feel him strangle me with it. I suppose by then I was unconscious.

Later, when the police were investigating my death, they discovered I'd been drugged with a powerful narcotic. It must have been in the champagne. I'd never drunk alcohol of any kind before, so how could I have known?

My body was found on an old bearskin hearth rug in the library of Gossington Hall, a country house in Radfordshire not far from the village of St Mary Mead. The case of 'The Body in the Library', as it came to be known, caused a great scandal in the surrounding area: the corpse of a murder victim, in a library of all places! Particularly when the library in question belonged to such upstanding members of the community as Colonel and Mrs Bantry, and when the corpse itself was so very … so very …

'Exotic' was the euphemism employed by the Chief Constable at the time, but everyone knew what he meant: that I looked, to put it bluntly, like a tart. Attractive, perhaps – beautiful, according to Mrs Bantry – but only in a way that was tawdry, and cheap, and vulgar. Even after the post-mortem medical examination established to politely unspoken surprise that I was 'virgo intacta', the idea that I might be the wholesome missing schoolgirl Pamela Reeves seemed ludicrous. I was identified instead as Ruby Keene, a professional dancer at the Majestic Hotel, who had also been reported missing. And when Ruby's charred remains were later discovered in a burned-out car, everyone assumed it was me.

Gerard and Josie killed us both. Ruby was about to deprive them of an inheritance they could not afford to lose; presenting my body as hers enabled them to set up an alibi covering the time of her disappearance, so no one could suspect them of any involvement. That was why Gerard had sought me out in the first place, although any other girl with a superficial resemblance to Ruby would have done just as well. I was a decoy, nothing more. He wasn't employed by Limeville Studios, he hadn't worked in Hollywood, and there was never going to be a film. Everything he told me was a lie. Even his name.

If the investigation had been left to the police, I would have been buried in a London graveyard with Ruby's name on my headstone, and she would have been buried in the Reeves family plot in

Danemouth, and no one would ever have known.

But Colonel and Mrs Bantry had a friend who did not believe in judging a book by its cover. Miss Marple saw past the superficial glamour of the body in the Gossington Hall library. She realised I could not be Ruby Keene, whatever Ruby's cousin Josie might have claimed, and step by step she established the truth. Because of her, Gerard and Josie were caught.

At his trial it made no difference that the crime had been entirely Josie's idea. It made no difference that she was secretly his wife and had more or less forced him to do it; if anything, the judge and jury only blamed him even more, for not standing up to her. Nor did it count for anything that he was sorry for killing me. After he was sentenced he wrote a letter to my parents to say so. My father refused to read it, and my mother tore it up.

He was hanged, of course. Murderers were, in those days.

At the far end of the Reference Library Reading Room is the Bristol Room, as far as possible a recreation of the reading room in the 1740 King Street library. It is dominated by a dark oak overmantel carved with flowers, fruit and game – the work of the eighteenth century woodcarver, Grinling Gibbons. The elaborate carving frames a portrait. But of whom? Both the subject and the painter are unknown.

The bookcases in the Bristol Room, as well as the overmantel, come from King Street. As for the tattered upholstered chair beside the fireplace, it is reputed to be the very chair in which Judge Jeffreys presided at the Bristol 'Bloody' Assize of 1685. Perhaps, because he lodged at King Street at the time.

Quick! Google it now!
We skim-read, and life flits by.
Take some time. Reflect.

Living Memory

Jenni O'Connor

Rachel gazed up at the soaring arches as she entered the library building. Which was it to be today, English or History? She had a lot of work to do for her A-Level History project on the early nineteenth century, with a special focus on social and economic transition, culminating in the abolition of slavery. Half of Bristol's grander buildings had been built with blood money, she knew – a thought which made her vaguely uncomfortable, now she stopped to think about it.

She sighed and picked up an unappealing tome which she thought would provide enough general background to get her going. Drily entitled *Britain in the Nineteenth Century*, its jacket, by contrast, featured a lurid battle scene. She gathered her files, pens and bag, and sat down to make notes.

As she started to read about the growing campaign to end slavery, led by William Wilberforce, her eyes fixed on an illustration. It was a roughly-sketched line drawing which looked as if it had been dashed off in a hurry, showing a girl of about eight bent over a broom, while a young woman mopped. Both were charcoal black, and despite their youth, their faces were worn. It was simply captioned: 'Bristol house slaves at work'. She hadn't realised slaves had also been brought to England.

She frowned and turned the page, scribbling '519 petitions before eventual abolition' on her notepad.

'Don't you flick past us like that!' A small voice piped up in the silence. 'What about OUR story?'

Rachel looked around, startled. 'What?' she asked. 'Who's there?'

A middle-aged lady at the next desk, who had been immersed in an academic-looking journal of some kind, glanced over enquiringly, dropping her gaze when Rachel's eyes met hers. Rachel coughed, embarrassed, realising she had spoken louder than she intended. There was no response, so she carried on reading. '… the industrial north provided the most enthusiastic support for abolition.'

'Turn back! Look at me!' It was the voice again, more insistent this time. Rachel tentatively returned to the sketch, as if the page might reveal a scuttling spider or biting ant. I'm going mad, she said to herself.

'No you're not,' said the voice, apparently reading her mind. 'I've been waiting for someone like you to open this book. It's been years, and nobody has touched it. It's very lonely, being stuck inside a book with no one to talk to.'

Rachel studied the portrait. 'Is that you? You look very young,' she whispered, trying to make it sound as if she was just reading key sentences aloud, for the benefit of her neighbour. 'Is the girl your daughter?'

'No, that's Dayo. I'm Ajeye. We were sold together. She's the reason I'm here … oh, never mind. I'll tell you in a minute. First things first. No, don't you go turning the page again, nah!'

The voice was getting impatient, and with it, easier – and harder – to place. It was not quite West Indian, nor the pastiche-Nigerian often heard on the telly.

'The reason I'm talking to you now,' it continued, 'is because while you're taking the time to make such detailed notes on Abolition – which was, of course, crucial to my survival, don't get me wrong – I just want you, or whoever is reading this book, to think about life before it, for a change. There. I've said it.'

Rachel looked back at the portrait, intrigued, feeling a chill – no, more of a tingle – creep up her spine. She was surprised to realise that she wasn't actually frightened, and that it suddenly felt quite natural to be having a conversation with a disembodied voice in a library book. 'So … who exactly are you?' she murmured. 'How did you get stuck in this book?'

The lady at the next desk looked up again and tutted, but Rachel ignored her.

'I came from Africa. Via the Caribbean. But I was sold here, in Bristol. And for my sins, I had to come back, even after I was freed. But I'm getting ahead of myself. It's been so long …'

'So you …?' Rachel looked down at the portrait, studying Ajeye's high cheekbones, sad oval eyes and grubby head wrap. In the picture, she was looking down at the little girl, her face a model of tenderness and regret which was visible despite the rough-drawn lines.

'Yes ma'am. Come with me and you will see …'

Rachel breathed in. The air changed. The library's studious, papery fug had been swept away by a gust of fresh salty air. The reigning silence was interrupted by men shouting brusque orders as a ship, named 'Abundance', crested the waves of a vast ocean.

'Close your eyes, lady, and imagine …'

Rachel could only obey. As her eyes got used to the gloom, she realised she was now in the hold of the ship. The ocean breeze had been replaced by a noxious blend of sweat and excrement, rum and sugar, salt and water. A slave ship! Row upon row of captives, packed tight as if in a mass grave, chained at the neck and ankles, each unable to move without disturbing the person next to him. Each bore festering lesions from the chains, and the stench was like nothing she had ever experienced. Not just the vile reek of month-old shit and vomit, but the sickly sweet odour of disease and death. She gagged, grabbing the table to stop herself from passing out.

And the sounds! Above the creak of the old wooden hull

straining against the sea, over the sound of the wind in the sails, she could hear an endless lament; an ongoing groan of pain and torment; the keening monotone of the living dead. It echoed round her head, not so much loud as insistent, and chilled her to the bone.

Looking farther in, she could see Ajeye, the young woman from the sketch. Someone next to her was trying to get her to eat. She was as thin and frail as a twig, eyes sunken in her cheeks, a suppurating sore oozing from her neck.

'Try some, go on,' cajoled the woman. Ajeye stared at the watered-down, maggoty slop for a long time. Eventually she put the rim of the cup to her lips and swallowed, her instinct to live evidently outweighing her desire to die.

'Everyone on deck! Now!' A horn blew, making Rachel jump, and seamen scuttled down the ladders to unchain the slaves. Ajeye complied, too exhausted to resist, as she was pushed and jostled up to the deck to dance with the rest of her section.

'You! Hop to it! Keep moving!' A sailor landed a cuff on her head, holding a broom for her to jump over. She tried to skip over it, staggered, and fell to the floor, curling up to shield herself from the kick which was bound to follow. Wearily she pulled herself up, just as a slave seized the moment of distraction to launch himself over the side of the ship, preferring the circling sharks to this living torture. Ajeye pressed her hands to her heart and up to her lips in a silent prayer for his soul.

Rachel shuddered, blinked and wiped her eyes, which were streaming with silent tears. When she looked down at the illustration again, Ajeye continued her story; it was as if she had been waiting for Rachel to catch up. 'But that was before we even reached Barbados,' she said. 'That woman you saw, who saved my life, was sold when we docked, along with most of the others. They were all probably dead within a year. But me? For some reason, they chose me, along with Olufemi and Dayo, and six or seven others, children and all, to go on another journey. I hoped we might be going home, but instead they sent us into a cold which froze the marrow in our bones …'

'Oi, you! Get a move on! You're lucky you weren't left with the others in the West Indies!'

As Rachel refocused her gaze, she saw Ajeye look up at her captors through unseeing eyes, seemingly immune to the torment of being prodded with a stick as she stumbled on the gangplank after what must have been a second transatlantic crossing locked in the boat's festering hold. Her dark skin had lost even more of its lustre and her eyes were pools of pain.

'Lucky? How dare you!' Ajeye muttered under her breath.

A man in a black woollen morning suit was waiting by a carriage at the dockside. The lapels of his coat folded back to reveal a white shirt with a high, frilly neck, and he wore a tall black hat. He carried a cane, and below his moustache his lips were cruel and thin. His eyes reminded Rachel of a dead fish.

He looked at Ajeye without speaking, then said to the sailor who had prodded her: 'She'll do. I'll take a man and a child, too.' He pointed with his cane. 'Him, and her.'

The sailor roughly disengaged a tall, very dark man and a girl of about eight, who Rachel recognised as the child from the sketch. One of the other women wailed as the child was pulled away, only to be struck in the face with a rifle butt. The girl froze, too frightened to cry, and was casually shoved towards the waiting carriage, slipping on the greasy cobbles on the way. Ajeye caught her as she stumbled and held her close, murmuring something in her ear which Rachel didn't catch, but which was clearly meant to reassure.

The man shrugged his shoulders, as if to shake off his captors, and walked to the carriage with his head high.

'You've got a right one there,' said the sailor to the man in the black suit, prodding the dark man towards the carriage steps. 'But it's your choice. You'll be wanting a receipt from the Captain.'

The vision faded. Rachel opened her eyes and came back into the familiarity of the library with a start, her head still spinning.

'And that was my new life,' said Ajeye sombrely. 'Sold. I was renamed Rachael, and taken to a draughty house to work until I died.'

'But my name's Rachel too!' Rachel blurted out, then stopped, embarrassed. As if that would make things better.

'Oho!' said Ajeye. 'I knew there was a reason I had to speak with you.'

Rachel smiled. 'And maybe I was waiting to meet you too,' she said.

'So, there I was. Not sitting nicely in your fine library, but being shoved into the carriage, with Olufemi, the man you saw just now, and Dayo, the little girl in the picture. You won't know this, but her name means Joy in Yoruba. They called him Edward and her Elizabeth, but we always remembered. Anyway, the carriage took us to a tall house in a square, but for all it looked nice-nice, it was cold inside, and there was no kindness there ...'

'Wash them down in the yard and get them in the cellar!' A male voice roared from the top of the stairs. 'I'll come and look at them later.'

'Yes, sir.' A fat woman in a frilly apron bobbed a curtsey, eyeing the new arrivals with suspicion. 'You!' she shouted to a thin girl in a ragged uniform, brandishing a frying pan. 'Earn your keep! Go and fetch some water and soap. And them old clothes as was left for 'em by Housekeeper. And get John from the stables, to keep an eye on 'em.'

'Yes, ma'am.' The thin girl scuttled off, looking apologetically over her shoulder, as if scared by her own shadow, soon reappearing with a bucket and a brutal-looking man armed with a horsewhip.

'You lot!' the man shouted, gesturing with the whip. 'Clothes off. Now!'

The slaves looked at each other, uncomprehending.

'Go on, before I take the frying pan to you all!' Cook mimed pulling her apron off.

Olufemi looked down the corridor, which led to a small door at the back of the house, and pointed hesitantly.

'Yes, yes. Now hurry up!'

Slowly the three arrivals made their way to the yard, prodded by the stable hand, and started to strip, covering their genitals. Olufemi was shaking. 'Barbarian sons of devils!' he muttered.

Ajeye screamed as a bucket of cold water was poured over her head. A stable boy had appeared in the yard and was enjoying the show, while John gazed openly at her shrivelled breasts.

'Enough of that noise,' shouted Cook, slapping her face. 'Here! Soap!'

Reluctantly, Ajeye reached for the tallow and lye block, grimacing as she caught its fatty smell.

'She's got a black cunny!' laughed the stable boy.

Ajeye shrank against the yard wall, holding on to Dayo and helping her to wash. Tears sprang to the little girl's eyes but Ajeye pressed a finger to her lips, fixing her captors with a defiant stare.

Olufemi remained motionless as another freezing bucket was emptied over him. He must have sensed the eyes of the thin wench on his scarred back, for he turned to glare at her from under lowered lids. 'For shame!' he spat.

'Well, at least you all smell better now,' declared Cook. 'Right, clothes on. Don't just stand there!'

The captives fumbled with the rough, unfamiliar garments, looking warily at each other.

'John! Alice!' – Cook gestured to the thin girl – 'Take them down to the cellar.'

'But I don't want to touch 'em, Cook,' complained Alice. 'You never know what they might 'ave.'

'You was 'appy enough to look, girl,' retorted Cook. 'And you don't know what you might get from me if you don't. Now come on! You lot! Down them stairs. Now!'

The cellar was dark. The man called John pushed them down the final few steps and in through the door, cursing as he went. Then he lit a candle, and in the flickering light Rachel could make out straw pallets to lie on.

'If it's good enough for my 'orses, it's good enough for you,' he declared. They may not have understood all his words, thought Rachel, but the sentiment was clear. The Africans held each other's hands as John stomped out, locking and bolting the door behind him. Dayo began to cry, uttering helpless, gasping sobs, and Ajeye held the girl against her chest, rocking her gently until her breathing calmed.

Rachel stared down at the portrait. 'How awful!' she whispered. 'I never thought ...'

'You people generally don't,' said Ajeye, not unkindly. 'You don't have to. And it was a long time ago. But still, you should try to understand ...'

'So what happened next?' asked Rachel.

'We were kept in that cellar, only unchained when we were doing tasks, or when they locked the door at night. Cook didn't want anything to do with us at first. She would open the door and shout at us to get up – we soon learned those words. They gave us some kind of porridge for breakfast, which tasted of paper and sludge and never left us full, but it was better than what we had to put up with on the ship. Then we were made to work from dawn until dark, seven days a week, with that horse man watching over us most of the time in case we tried to escape. He was a vicious bastard. Even little Dayo was sweeping out the hearths, fetching and carrying. Sometimes the Master would come and see that he was getting his money's worth from us, sitting and sketching while we worked in the house, as if we were his entertainment – yes, he did that drawing in the book. And poor Olufemi was treated like a pack horse.'

She paused, reflecting. 'It is a sad thing, to see a proud man beaten into the ground. Over time, his eyes lost the gleam I remembered him by, and he cast them down when anyone spoke to him, to keep out of trouble.

'We were all sick from overwork, cold and new diseases. The coughs and colds got into our lungs, made worse by the smoke and smog. You would have thought they would take better care of their investment, nah, especially as their goal was to sell us on as servants. Highly fashionable at the time, ma'am, if we could learn the harsh sounds of your language well enough. Which we did, in time, of course.'

'And were you? Sold on, I mean?'

'Ah, that's what I was coming to. Patience, lady, patience!'

'It's not right.' Cook was in the kitchen, stirring a huge pot of soup.

'What's not?' The thin girl, Alice, looked up from her ironing.

'Them lot. Elizabeth. Edward. Rachael. I mean, for starters, them's not their names, are they? Can you imagine? Being taken away from where you were born, from your kin, put on a ship, and made to work for nothing.'

'But them's just savages. They don't know any different.'

'Don't they? When I hear them talking – now their English is better – I think they knows a lot they doesn't let on. And now I'm used to looking at them, well …' she paused. 'I saw Rachael smile the other day. She was singing to herself, in her language, didn't know I was there. Made me realise how sad and lonely she looks, the rest of the time. And how frightened the nipper is. Even now they've got proper beds and aren't chained up any more. There's a fear in her eyes, even though she don't say much. And they're poorly most of the time. Even if I try to give them a bit more food than Housekeeper allows.'

'You all right?' asked Cook, bustling in as Ajeye spluttered over the sooty hearth.

Ajeye shook her head. 'The cold's got into my chest and this cough never goes away. And now Dayo has a fever. She's hot-hot and talking nonsense in her sleep. I'm so worried.'

Ajeye's eyes were ringed with shadows and Rachel could see she hadn't got much rest the previous night.

'They should call a doctor in,' said Cook, patting her arm. 'It's criminal.'

Ajeye gave a wan smile. 'I will be fine. I just hope Dayo will get better. I wish we could go … home.'

'Fat chance of that!' snorted Cook, but there was compassion in her eyes. 'I'll see if I can find something for the poor girl.' She busied herself in a cupboard, then handed Ajeye a packet of powder. 'This'll help. Put it in water for her.' She brought a glass. 'Where you come from, what's it like, then?'

Ajeye sighed as she summoned her memories. 'The sun shines so brightly, and the trees are so green. The sky here is never blue like it is at home, and it is warm, even when it rains. And we have fruit! Fruit like you 'as never seen here. I don't know your names for our fruit, but they are sweet, with juice that makes you hungry for more.'

She shrugged her thin shoulders. 'You know what makes me sad, Cook? So much time has passed, I find it hard to remember. The sun, the sky, the trees … they are all fading. Even in my dreams, I see your land rather than ours.'

Cook squeezed her hand. 'I'm sorry,' she said softly.

'It's not your fault,' said Ajeye. 'But I miss my parents, my sister, the man I loved. I think about them every day, but I find it hard to see their faces now.' Her voice tailed off, then rallied. 'Our tribe, they didn't take people. I know some other tribes captured our brothers and sisters, they sold them to the white men on the boats. But our people refused to do that. Our people always believed in talking to solve problems, not fighting. That's why so many of us were caught. My man was taken not long before I was, when he went down to the river to fish. I'll never know …' she wiped a tear from her cheek. 'And Dayo lost her mother on that ship. Can you imagine, Cook, losing everything and everyone you love?'

Rachel sat very still, taking in all she had seen. When she closed her eyes again, she saw Ajeye, who was sitting by Dayo's bed in a rare moment of repose, sponging her forehead and singing tenderly to her. Cook came into the room.

'Is she any better?' she asked.

'I think a little,' said Ajeye. 'But only time will tell.'

'Come downstairs a minute, there's someone as wants to meet you.'

Ajeye kissed Dayo on the cheek and struggled to her feet. 'But nobody comes for me,' she said suspiciously. Cook touched her finger to her nose, and then to her lips to indicate silence, and the two women slipped down to the back door. A man was waiting with a delivery of bread.

'If you'll just take these,' the man said loudly.

Ajeye looked puzzled, but went to pick up the loaves.

'He's my cousin,' said Cook in a loud whisper. 'Been helping some of your kind since he came here from London a few months back. I mentioned you lot to him the other day. He has an idea.'

Rachel looked at the portrait in the book, eyes wide. 'So you escaped? Cook's cousin helped you?'

'Something like that,' said Ajeye. 'Cook was a good woman, you know, for all she didn't like us at first, and her cousin had become involved with those Abolitionists you're reading about – no, don't turn the page yet! – a year or so after we arrived.'

'So he smuggled you all out?'

'Not quite all.' Ajeye sighed. 'That was why I had to come back. He said he could take me and Olufemi, but not Dayo, because she was too sick to travel. It would make it too dangerous.' There was a long silence, followed by a muted sob. 'I – we – decided to leave her. It was the hardest thing I ever did, leaving that little girl. She was like my daughter. But Cook said she'd take care of her, make sure our escape didn't get taken out on her, and I believed her. And so we went.'

'Where?'

'London. Abolition wasn't far off by then, and Cook's cousin had contacts there, so we had a good chance of getting a job without being challenged. The tide had turned, and for every filthy slave-owner – God rot them all – there was somebody prepared to help. Usually ordinary folk like Cook. So we were all right. In the end.'

'And Dayo? Did you ever hear?'

There was a small silence. 'She died,' said Ajeye bleakly. 'Cook sent word a few weeks after we left. She did her best, convinced the Master to call a doctor, but there was nothing anyone could do.' She paused. 'I never forgave myself. I shouldn't have let her die alone, with none of her people to bury her.'

Rachel found herself stroking the woman's forehead in the picture. 'It wasn't your fault.'

'No, I couldn't help her getting ill. But I could have waited. Freedom called us with such a strong voice. So anyway, that's why I came back. To find her memory in that silly sketch the Master drew. So we can stay together.'

Ajeye sighed. 'It's time for me to go now. I'm losing my strength. I just needed someone – you – to know. I'm very glad it was you. Please don't forget us.'

Rachel sat back in her chair, unable to process what had just happened. She was shaking, and wanted to cry, but no tears came.

She strained her ears for more words from Ajeye, but silence had returned, and the foul stench of the docks had been replaced with the studious mustiness of books. Returning the book she had borrowed to its shelf, she suddenly knew exactly what she had to write.

The 1967 extension to the Central Library was designed by the City Architect Albert H Clarke to give a modern echo to the 1906 library but the finished building was modified and did not include the third floor he had planned.

Sitting at my desk
waiting for inspiration.
Lives reinvented.

Inside The Van

Nina Milton

I was brought up on the old films, black and white. They filled my teenaged afternoons. I must have always known about myself, because I liked the mental asylum ones the best. Bars at the windows, like a prison. Strange treatments for mad folk. People in white jackets, cross-armed and mashed into a corner.

They don't do those rooms nowadays. Not for fifty years at least. It's just 'put you out', nighty-night and good luck. They even pin you down different, taking care how you're held, how you're squeezed. They smile as you drift off. It's all very civilised. Got to be – done by example. They want you to be civilised nowadays.

I was expecting different, when it finally happened. I heard Sandra on the other side of the door, tapping, quiet at first, 'Simon?' then louder, till the panic in her seeped through and made me angry, a pain searing down from my scalp, like I was splitting in two.

Then there was proper banging and the door caved in, and there were legs, and arms like windmills, and faces, right up close. I was expecting to be thrown into a room from which there was no escape and no chance of destruction. I'd almost been hoping. Instead, there was the gentle pinning, like I was a moth about to be etherised – don't break an antenna or anything – and once I was displayed on cork, not able to fend off the little scratch, it was nighty-night, the civilised smiles blurring as I slid down, down, into drift-off.

I wished they still had the rooms. And then, I was introduced to the van.

I didn't want the driving job, but they try to find you something, force you to have a go.

I'd been longing to be left alone where the edges wouldn't catch. Silence. No gabble. No gabbling sessions in a circle. 'Please don't speak all at once,' Lois would say. 'Simon, would you like to say something?'

'No thank you, Lois.'

'You have nothing on your mind?'

She knew the answer. No point in asking a question if you know the answer.

If I'd started up with the gabble … well, it wouldn't have been civilised, put it like that. It would have been hyper-gabble. My mind is full of somethings to say. Overloaded with them. Silence is the solution.

Outside, the van has metal walls. When I walked around its outside, the gabble was still in my head. But inside, the walls are cushioned. Lined with paper. Soft, and lined with silence. The books are thick with so many leaves of paper you couldn't count. I certainly won't count. I keep them closed.

I drive the country lanes, down tracks and through gushing fords. I can hear the birds singing, but no gabbling. I stop on the corner by the village shop. There is already a bunch of people waiting. I open the doors and get out of the driving seat and squeeze behind the little desk ready to do the stamping. The people climb in silently, nodding to me. They understand the no talking rule. They stand at the walls, muted with book after book, touching the spines with the pad of a finger. Occasionally they pull one out like a loose tooth. Some flick through. Others seem to read the entire thing then put it back. I don't care what they do, so long as they don't gabble.

One by one they check their watches and bring their choices to me. They might whisper something, but it's not gabble. It's reverent, that's what it is. 'Will you be getting the full Booker shortlist?' they might ask. Or, 'Can I renew this one please?'

I open the book at the front page, where there is whiteness and silence. Just a label, ready to be stamped.

Finally, they've gone. I lean into the cab and close the doors.

For a few moments I won't drive off. I like to have the room to myself.

I like to listen to the padded silence of the walls of books. It's ironic, I always think, because if I opened any one of those books, gabble would come teeming out. Words by the thousands, millions, leaping into my head. Some words would be civilised to the highest degree. Others would be boorish or gross or even barbaric in their speech, like the gabblers who shouted over everyone else, even Lois.

She liked words, did Lois. She explained to me that they did away with the padded cells because therapy worked so much better. 'Talk away the fears, Simon,' she used to say.

Sometimes, I hear her whisper in my ear. 'Open a book and read, Simon. Go on … go on …'

Sometimes I touch a spine and wonder. Bronte, it might say. Archer, Fielding. Murdoch. Cartland. I do wonder.

But I never look. I just get in the cab and drive the van to the next parking place.

A café and a galleon (for the children's section) are part of today's Central Library. You can borrow DVDs and CDs; there are e-books and there's Internet access. And more: as well as the branch and mobile libraries there's an at-home service for the housebound, and there's the twenty-four hour online library.

As for the books, they are all unchained now.

The world fades. High walls
of books block out distraction,
chaos, clamour, life.

Reasonable Adjustments

Ali Bacon

R oy frowned as he heard the murmur of voices in the corridor outside. Callers up here in the topmost part of the library were rare. Then came the tentative knock, the head around the door, the smile that offered token professional bonhomie. Jason Lee, Reference Librarian, turned to usher in a waif-like creature who preferred to loiter behind him in the doorway.

'Hello Roy,' Jason said. 'Just brought up a visitor. Wondered if you could do the honours?'

With Jason standing aside, the girl had no option but to walk forward into the room. She was, Roy thought, shockingly young, no more than fourteen or fifteen. Her eyes were rimmed in black, the lashes daubed into thick spikes against pale green eyelids.

'Kelly's with the group from St. Jude's,' Jason said. 'I mentioned it at the meeting?'

Now that his hours had been cut, Roy missed the weekly staff briefing, but he did read the emailed notes. Jason couldn't catch him out on that. The girl was on work experience, although school uniform clearly wasn't *de rigueur*. She wore grotesque trainers, tight black jeans and a shapeless white jumper that drooped off one shoulder to reveal an orange T-shirt underneath. 'Kelly's finished her task for this morning,' Jason said, 'and said she'd like to see more of the library. Do you have a minute to show her round up here?'

'You mean now?' he asked.

It must have come out more sharply than Roy intended because the girl jumped.

'If it's not too much trouble,' Jason said. 'Shall we say twenty minutes? Then she can rejoin her group for lunch. You're the expert, after all.'

Jason was wily, playing to Roy's knowledge of the nooks and crannies of the old building. But whatever his agenda, it wasn't the girl's fault. She was giving Roy a cautious smile. He placed the book he'd been processing back on to the pile. 'OK,' he said, 'let's see what we can do.'

The office had a door at each end. Kelly guessed it had once been a corridor. A grey cardigan hung from a hook on the far door and in the corner, underneath the shelf with the kettle and the tea-stained mug, there was a plastic carrier with a newspaper and a lunchbox poking out. The old-fashioned lights made everything (the tatty poster of an exhibition, the piles of books on the floor and Mr Stanbrook himself) a pasty yellow, a colour that went with the niff of old man's sweat. At least she thought that's what it was. But although the old man had made her jump, he wasn't scary. When creepy Jason left, the librarian took off the green visor he'd been wearing and laid it on his desk.

'What's that for then?' she said.

He blinked at her and she thought she was in for a telling-off, then he seemed to change his mind. 'I have problems with my eyes. Especially when I use a screen.' He got up and shuffled towards the far door.

'You got bad legs too, then?'

He stood back to let her go ahead of him. 'Yes. I have diabetes. It affects lots of things.'

That figured. Lonely and not very well. 'My gran has diabetes. It must be hard for you working up here, with all them stairs?'

'This is where my work is, checking the old stock and transferring records to the computer system. And they've put in a lift now.'

Outside they stood in the corner of a kind of balcony that ran around the main reading room. Mr Stanbrook was telling her the books up here were the oldest in the library. Kelly ignored him and stepped forward to look over the parapet. Below them people sat at the library tables, hunched over notepads and laptops, or just slobbing out, heads thrown back and stuff strewn around them, as if taking up space was what mattered.

'I bet you see all sorts from up here,' she said. 'You can be invisible.' He was closer behind her than she had realised. She could feel his breath on her hair.

'And do you like being invisible?' he said.

She shrugged. 'They kept giving me rubbish jobs. Making posters and stuff. I said wasn't there a proper library somewhere?'

The rest of the school group had assembled halfway down the Reading Room with the lady librarian in charge. 'Look,' she said. 'There's Jason … and … Miss Marshall.'

Jason's boss had said they could call her Liz, but Mr S might not go along with that. Kelly had liked her straight away. She didn't look anything like the librarian at school. Her make-up was good and she had nice perfume, really flowery but not OTT. When she spoke to the kids they answered her properly, not giving cheek or anything. As Kelly watched, Liz glanced up to the balcony as if something had caught her eye. Kelly waggled her fingers in a wave, but the librarian didn't seem to notice.

Mr Stanbrook had moved away but his breathing was still noisy. Maybe he had asthma as well as everything else.

'We'd better get on with the tour,' he said.

He led her along the shelves, explaining the numbering system and showing her some cranky old machinery for moving books up and down the floors.

'Does it still work?'

'Maybe, but it isn't used any more. Not safe, apparently.'

'So how do they move the books?'

'The books up here are hardly ever asked for.'

'So why do they keep them?'

'Because someone might need them, one day.'

Mr Stanbrook was getting tetchy. He was like one of these old books that didn't often get read. Jason must be hanging on to him, just on the offchance he'd come in useful.

The girl was asking too many questions, and even when she didn't her voice rose at the end of every sentence in that annoying way. Roy was beginning to wish he hadn't agreed to show her round. And he no longer liked looking down on the world below, not since he'd noticed how people behaved when they thought they couldn't be seen: ducking into corners, gossiping, having a bit of a canoodle.

'Time to get back,' he said.

The girl stopped short. 'What's that then?'

In a space on one of the shelves, just at eye level, there was a yellow slip. The sight of it brought a stab of nostalgia. At one time, before computers took over, these slips had been the only system there was, one layer peeled off and stuck in the book as it was taken to the Reading Room, the other left on the shelf to signify it had gone. This one was weighed down by a green biro placed across it at a careful angle. Something about the pen and the way it lay stirred a memory.

The girl went over to look at it but didn't pick it up.

'What does it say?' he said.

She read out the book title and the Dewey number from the slip. It would do no harm to let her see how things used to work. 'Can you find the book on the shelf?'

As she picked up the pen and the slip underneath it Roy saw

how it left a clear space, an empty rectangle, in the surrounding dust.

Kelly was perusing the shelves. 'It should be here, but I can't see it,' she said.

The memory was more insistent now. A grown woman rather than a girl, but with the same curiosity, eyes that met his, head on.

The teenager was poking the spines with the pen, biting her Cupid's bow lips in concentration. 'They're in alphabetical order, aren't they? This one's MIT, but it's not here. They go straight from MAS to MOR.'

'Is there a date on the slip?'

The eyes flickered in disappointment. '1995. It's ancient. How come it's still here?'

'It must have been forgotten. Whoever wanted it probably gave up looking.' Or preferred not to come back. He glanced over the parapet to see if anyone was watching.

In the office Mr Stanbrook went over to a cabinet like the one her sister Emma kept jewellery in, but bigger and more solid. It was made up of drawers, each drawer with a label on the front in a metal holder. He opened the drawer for 'M' and showed Kelly the card that matched the yellow slip from 1995, still in her hand.

'This is the catalogue entry for your book.'

She liked the way he called it hers, even if she had never seen it. 'What happens now?'

He slid out a metal rod from the drawer, removed the card and wrote 'missing' on the top in pencil, then placed it on a pile on the corner of his desk. 'I'll check to see if there's a computer record. If there is, I'll delete it. Then everything will be tidy.'

'So no one will ever know it was here?'

He sat down and put his green visor back on. She'd been going to ask him if he'd have any use for that cabinet once everything was on the computer. It would be so cool in her bedroom. But it looked like her time was up.

'I'd best get back then. Thanks for the tour, Mr Stanbrook.'

As she went downstairs she found she still had the slip in her hand. She was examining it when she bumped into the rest of the group. Liz, the boss lady, took it from her.

'Here's a curiosity,' she said to the others.

Roy recognised the knock. Not that she waited for an answer, but then why should she? She was Head of Reader Services now.

She stood in front of him. 'Hello Roy. How are you?'

He didn't look up from his work but he caught her fragrance, subtle, alluring. This must be what they meant by expensive. Liz Marshall ignored the fact he hadn't replied. 'That work-experience girl, the bright one. She reminded me of something.'

He could see she was holding a book, front cover towards him. *Mitchell's Commentary on St. Paul.* The crumpled yellow slip stuck up from between its pages. She had the book, the missing book. Something did not compute.

'You mean you had it all along?'

She shook her head. 'Not exactly my cup of tea, is it? I must have found it afterwards and the slip just got forgotten.' Afterwards. So she did remember. 'If you must know it's been propping up my PC for the last three years.'

The hem of her skirt fell just below her knee to the top of her high-heeled leather boots. On the day they'd found themselves alone in Bible Commentaries she'd been wearing tight black trousers ending in shiny pink pumps. Shocking pink, like her jumper. A stick of candyfloss. He could taste her lipstick now on his tongue. And hear the footsteps, the suppressed laughter from below.

She was still offering the book to him. He pulled his visor down to cut out the glare of memory. 'Couldn't you have used a computer stand?'

Silence. No more than he deserved. For weeks afterwards he had skulked in different parts of the book stacks. But no one had come. She had never made a complaint. Sometimes he thought if she had it would have been easier. Skulking had become a habit.

'We don't see much of you downstairs these days,' she said, as if reading his thoughts.

'It's best I keep out of the way. I know I'm ...'

'Expendable? Come on, Roy. We've already made the reasonable adjustments. And we need all the staff we've got these days. You're wasted up here.'

He took off his visor, laid it down and met her eye. He might have ruffled her composure at twenty-two but she had always had confidence. At forty she had gained compassion, or maybe she was just doing her job. Either way, there was no need to apologise.

'Thanks for the book,' he said.

She was smiling now. 'No problem, Roy.'

On Friday, her last day, Kelly saw Mr Stanbrook in the downstairs corridor and thanked him. He raised his eyebrows in a question. 'For giving me "very good" on my feedback. Jason only gave me "satisfactory".'

'That's all right. You deserved it.'

She had no idea why. 'I gave that slip to Miss Marshall. Do you know she had that book all along?'

'Yes, she told me.'

'It wasn't lost after all, was it? Did you take it off your computer?'

'No, I didn't. Sometimes things go missing then turn up again. Sometimes it's good to give them another chance.'

He was walking with less of a stoop and his hair looked fluffier than before. Maybe he'd got new tablets or something. He gave her a wavery smile and shuffled off.

Reference Library

Shirley Wright

Here is the dark half-world
where roots weave earth
tight against the spin, the turn
of leaves, where night

owls swoop on echoes
from the wildwood, a vole perhaps,
the musk of history, things
dank or rustling.

Heads bow as though
to avoid the casual swipe
of low branches, the crack
and biro-click that herald

autumnal fruit. See
how it is garnered, one word,
one phrase at a time, acorns
in a grove of oaks from whence

all this transfigured landscape
had its being. Chairs creak,
tables groan beneath their load
of elbows and narrow fingers .

fingering the black and white;
we might pause for coffee,
whisper thoughts on metempsychosis,
pick mushrooms from the forest floor.

Bristol Women Writers
Author Biographies

Ali Bacon

Ali moved to Bristol in the 1970s after graduating from St. Andrews University. Here she worked in libraries of all shapes and sizes (the eagle-eyed might spot a few of them in her fiction) until the writing bug finally bit. Her first novel was shortlisted for the A&C Black First Novel Award 2007. Her second, *A Kettle of Fish*, was published last year by ThornBerry Publishing. Also a blogger and book reviewer, she now spends too much time on social media while grappling with the occasional short story and a novel set in Victorian Edinburgh. http://alibacon.com

Nicola Bennetts

Nicola is currently working on a biography, though her writing to date has been freelance journalism and selling to magazines and broadsheets, most recently the *Financial Times*. The inspiration behind her anthology entry was a true story told to her by the late Arthur Negus. As for the snippets of Library history, they are distilled from *Bristol Central Library and Charles Holden* by Anthony Beeson together with a behind-the-scenes tour by Andrew Cox, the Reading Manager at the Library.

Jean Burnett

A lifelong bookworm and secret scribbler, Jean now occasionally gets paid to write. She studied at Exeter and Cardiff Universities and, after her marriage, lived in the USA, Canada and Mexico. Here in Bristol she has taught creative writing and did freelance journalism and advertising copywriting. Following a year off to see the world she published the travel book *Vagabond Shoes*, which won the book prize at Winchester Writers' Conference. Her novel, *Who Needs Mr. Darcy?* was published in 2012 by Little, Brown. She is currently writing a sequel and also has a historical novel looking for a home. www.jeanburnett.co.uk

Louise Gethin

Born and brought up in Bristol, Louise Gethin writes short fiction for adults. She explores birth, love, death and everything in between. This year, her collection *Anecdotes of Love and Death* will be published online. She has performed her work as part of the Word of Mouth series and on The Review Show, Bristol Community Radio. A graduate of the MA in Creative Writing at Bath Spa University College, Louise has won prizes for her short fiction at Winchester Writers' Conference, been shortlisted for the Mslexia short story prize and longlisted for the Bristol Short Story Prize.

Sally Hare

Sally completed the Bath Spa Creative Writing MA in 2006 and more recently undertook an eighteen month mentorship with the writer in residence at Exeter University. She is currently working on her third novel, and would not have completed nearly as much without the encouragement and support of the group members listed here. Extended fiction is her preferred genre, though she occasionally tries her hand at short stories and articles. A former pier-end novelty seller, reflexologist and carer support worker, teaching belly dancing when nine months pregnant has been one of her more interesting choices of career.

Jane Jones

After leaving university Jane spent a couple of very tedious years working in financial services before training as a secondary school English teacher. Her last (as yet unpublished) novel, written in odd moments squeezed between paid work and the demands of raising a family, took ten years to complete; she hopes to finish the current one in less than half that time. A big fan of the classic English whodunit, she sees her own work as an updating of that tradition. Coincidentally, but very conveniently, she married a forensic toxicologist.

Nina Milton

Nina was born, educated and raised her two children in the watery city of Bristol, but now lives in Wales and grows her own veg with husband, James. She is a prize-winning short story writer, and the author of several children's books. She holds an MA in creative writing, and works as a tutor and writer for the Open College of the Arts. Her most recent creation is the Shaman Series, which are fast-paced thrillers fusing earth magic and crime action. The first novel, *In the Moors*, was published by Midnight Ink in August 2013. http://www.kitchentablewriters.blogspot.com

Jenni O'Connor

Jenni has a passion for writing, and has worked as a journalist and copywriter, as well as writing fiction and haiku poetry. Inspired by her time in the Caribbean, she has written a novel set in post-Independence Jamaica called *Reach for a Different Sun*, which was a quarter-finalist in the 2012 Amazon Breakthrough Novel Award. She has also written a travel narrative set in the region, currently lodged in a drawer, called *Turn Left by the Coconut Vendor*. After leaving work to start her family, Jenni set up her own company,

Kaiku Communications, specialising in copywriting for print and web.

Gail Swann

Gail is an owner/director of a Bath-based graphic design company and mum to two teenage girls. She completed a novel, *One Of The Few*, landing herself an agent and some flattering rejections before conceding to the demands of babies and business for a few years. This 'midnight oil' period produced an assortment of shorter work but she lacked the time to try and do anything with it! Gail is now full steam ahead on a brand new novel and is also co-ordinating the Unchained project and the BWW group's emergence into a more public light (and hopefully, her own!).

Shirley Wright

Shirley is a poet and author. She has various short stories in print, and last year her novel *Time out of Mind* was published by ThornBerry Publishing. In 2008 she was the national winner of the Telegraph/Rose Theatre Poetry for Performance Competition, judged by the (then) Poet Laureate, Andrew Motion. More recently in Oct 2012 she won second prize in the Wells International Poetry Competition with 'Reference Library' which was specifically written for this anthology. Her first poetry collection *The Last Green Field* was published by Indigo Dreams in the summer of this year. http://sswright.webplus.net